# My Universe

*By*

*Chris Flores*

# Dedication

Dedicated to a woman who will always remain priceless. A woman's worth goes beyond pay and what she brings. A woman's worth, in general, is priceless. Far be it a man to decide her worth when her worth was already there. Her worth is more valuable than any precious metal found on this earth. Her worth lies in her virtue, honesty, loyalty, love, and devotion to him. Her worth is no currency; it is something that is immeasurable. Her worth is seen by only the right man, and for the man that sees her true worth, he is truly the richest man alive, for the two of them are now made whole.

# Acknowledgment

Cover art by Katherine Chandler

# About the Author

Chris Flores (1974- ) was born in Midland, Texas, and moved to San Antonio shortly after the oil crash in 1986. What started out as a hobby, turned into a passion that he has pursued since the death of wife in 2009. He has published two books, one being about true events of his childhood upbringing, and the other book being a romance novel dedicated to his late wife. Mr. Flores is passionate about the aspects of human emotion and expresses it freely and intensely because so many have lost touch within themselves and with others.

# Table of Contents

*She is my church, my place of worship.*

*One hundred percent. That's a number that should never exist when it comes to a relationship. I don't want one hundred percent. That number is achievable without effort. I want your breath, your heart, your soul, your eyes, your touch, your love, and your body. After all that, I want your thoughts, your fears, your dreams, your sadness, and your hopes. I want infinite for eternity.*

**—Chris Flores**

# **Destined**

Somewhere it is written that when two people meet, they know they are destined to be with each other. It may take many years or a lifetime for that one person to come along, and you may share a lifetime that is truly remarkable or even the last few seconds that can replace a lifetime of loneliness.

When I met the one, I at first saw her in a lowly strip club. She stared in silent devotion at a candle with but only a tiny flame. Nothing else mattered to her, but that barely lit flame. With all that surrounded the two of us that night, nothing was more void than the outside world.

Her insignificant flame flickered back and forth, but she didn't break her silent stare.

My flame was an unknown individual who also flickered back and forth, almost going out, but she did just enough to breathe.

My flame, the one who was near breathless, was married to another, and that was enough for me to walk away. But it wasn't enough for her since she would cross oceans to find me and give me all of herself. But none of this would be possible without Nia.

Nia is my most trusted friend and colleague, and now the CEO of BlackStone, the world's most powerful company, which I founded more than thirty years ago.

Nia had only one question for Sky. One question. Just one.

"How do you know you love him?"

"Because I can hear his heartbeat."

Without hesitation, Nia placed Sky on a plane and flew her to me.

With Sky possessing everything that I could ever want, I promised never to let her go and to devote my entire life to her—a life of utter happiness, a life so filled with love it would spill over to the afterlife.

*Never will your flame burn so low, never will you be alone, never, until my last breath.*

*I will show you everything for the rest of my life and share with the world that you are the most precious gift ever to be given to me. I unwrap you with loving care and hold you unconditionally.*

# The Beginning

The waves crash hard against the cliff.

*The sun shines down on your radiance, and your hair flows ever so gracefully in the wind. We stand together atop a cliff in England, overlooking the Atlantic Ocean.*

As Nia stands with Sky, they both smile down at the individual standing next to me. I look down at my beloved chow mix dog named Mena, who smiles with her purple tongue hanging out, adoring Sky with her eyes.

Sky smiles at me. I smile back at her since I know the rest of our lives are about to begin. I anxiously wait for the words.

I begin to hear words that I haven't heard in quite some time. But as I hear them being spoken, I begin to realize how much I have missed loving someone this much.

*But you are not just someone. You are my universe.*

*You are the moon, the stars, the planets, the cosmos, the galaxies, and everything else that could possibly exist. You are the reason why love stories are told. You are the reason for happy endings. You are the reason for laughter and heartfelt emotions.*

*With all these reasons, there is one reason that counts the most. You. You are my reason. You are my beginning and my end.*

I begin to tremble in anticipation.

Alas, the final words are said.

*I finally get to unveil you. I reach for your veil and slowly pull it back. I have seen your face countless times, and still, such beauty could never be imagined.*

*When I look into your eyes, I see a world in which I can only belong. I touch the side of your face. You are soft, you are breathless, and most importantly, you are mine.*

*I kiss you, and from within, a seal is broken.*

For so long, this seal contained what I have always wanted to give the one I love. It flows throughout, it flows in a rush, it surges, and it crushes anything in its path.

*I am ready to start this life with you. I will show you love and devotion like no other. Till the end of time, I will forever belong to you.*

*Now, my love, let us begin our story, a story that will be for the ages.*

I am pleased to introduce my readers to Mrs. Sky Branch.

# Pure Beauty

*I see you getting dressed from afar. I see your beautiful face as you look in the mirror. Your reflection is that of an angel. With my eyes, I follow your hair as it is stroked to one side. My lips are wet; I see how beautiful you are. My eyes slowly travel down the side of your neck and down your left shoulder.*

*Your natural curves make you so irresistible. Your natural backside is a gift from the heavens above. I close my eyes and invite those sensual thoughts to fill my head. I open them, hoping I am not dreaming, that you truly are here with me.*

*My heart races as I realize you are no dream, but you are the most beautiful woman I have ever laid eyes on. I continue my travel down your legs. Your legs go for miles. I travel your natural highway of beauty with desire.*

*When a bright light flashes, I am blinded for a second. The sparkle on your left-hand does you no justice, but you were never one for materialistic things. Too bad I am, and I want to give you the world.*

*I begin my journey to you.*

*Your natural gravity sinks into my body. I do not fight it; instead, I invite the collision of your tremendous beauty. I am only a few steps away, and I can smell your beauty. I let the smell of you course through my body.*

*The anticipation is overwhelming. If only your gravity of undeniable love could draw me in faster. Please latch on to me harder and never let go.*

*I am almost there.*

*I am almost to you.*

*I am almost home.*

*I reach for you. The tips of my fingers begin to tingle; my body shakes as contact is made. An immense explosion felt between our bodies. The Earth shakes, bodies of water tremble, and the winds howl in delight.*

*I embrace this impact of two heavenly bodies only made for each other.*

*I hold on to you.*

*I caress you.*

*I protect you.*

# Stand Guard

I am wide awake with darkness as my only friend. When I turn my head, I see something that makes me sad and alone.

*The ticks of the clock slowly take you away from me.*

The stages of sadness begin their course.

*I turn and look at you.*

*You are an angel breathing ever so quietly in this darkness. While you are only a few inches away from me, you might as well be a world away.*

Time is my enemy right now, and there's no way to win this fight.

*I watch you sleep ever so peacefully. I look at every inch of your face. I count every eyelash you have. I memorize every part of your face, and I engrain your perfectly lined lips in my head.*

*I reach for a strand of hair that covers your beauty.*

I am no painter, but with one simple stroke, I witness perfection.

*You are a portrait of endless beauty.*

Painters and artists could never achieve this beautiful perfection in their lifetime.

*The ticks of time are at the gate and about to enter and disrupt our world. Nevertheless, I will defend you till my last breath. Time may take you away from me.*

*But I will rage.*

*Rage.*

*Rage.*

*Stand behind me, my love, and watch how love is truly defined.*

*But before this battle starts, let me look at you one last time. Let me take these last few seconds and gaze upon you, my Queen. Let my heart and mind be full of you, my love, and let this King's last stand make you proud.*

The sound of war is triggered.

Gesture, the world's most advanced AI personal assistant rings the alarm with a subtle chime.

I ask Gesture to silence the alarm.

Sky is awakened. She turns to me.

"My love," she says, "stay ten more minutes."

She buries her face in my chest and goes back to sleep. While I am victorious in battle, the war is not yet won.

I reach down and touch her hair softly.

"Yes, my love," I say, "ten minutes."

I will spend those ten minutes touching my universe, touching her hair softly, and smelling her beautiful scent as she lies on top of me.

I look at the clock. Again, the countdown has begun, and again, I will stand guard.

# I Love You

There is a lot of chatter, laughter, and drinking among our friends, who are like family. I sit on the opposite end of Sky. I am in conversation after conversation, but my eyes always search for her. I love her smile, I love her hand gestures, and that little thing she does when she pushes a strand of hair behind her ear.

My Queen is radiant tonight. Her laughter is inviting and contagious. I could look at her all night and never get tired of such beauty. She is the first face I see and the last face I think about. I will lend my ears this evening but not my eyes. They belong to her.

She takes a sip of her red wine. Why couldn't I be that glass? Why do I envy a glass?

Why must a King sit opposite his Queen? Who would make such a ridiculous rule? She is to sit next to her King.

I am trying my best to keep myself reserved and calm. I am a volcano waiting to erupt if I cannot have her by my side. But suddenly, she does something that is only shared between us.

In the feline kingdom, when an animal slowly closes its eyes and then slowly opens them, it is saying, "I love you."

She looks at me. Time begins to slow. She smiles. She slowly closes her eyes.

She slowly opens them to me.

A private moment of love between us.

A moment that lasts all of one second. But I will take that one second and make it last a lifetime.

I crave her, desire her, and need her with me.

Her eyes calm me.

Her eyes settle on me.

Her eyes tell me, "I love you."

I smile at my Queen.

I slowly whisper, "I love you too."

# A Powerful Love

The night life in Singapore is extravagant and alive. We sit on the roof of the hotel with some of the world's finest restaurants, but she insists on making dinner for the two of us on this night. The view is truly magnificent, but as I come in from the balcony, I realize nothing could ever be as beautiful as my universe.

She is cutting vegetables in the kitchen. The knife cuts evenly and gracefully. Only she could make it look like an art form. The recessed lights from above create a halo above her head as if she were the chosen one. But wait, she is. She is my chosen one.

She's wearing a simple white cotton t-shirt and black shorts. While her clothes are simple, she is absolutely stunning, with red carpet worthiness. Her skin is as soft as a gentle breeze, her hair shines with magnificence, and her eyes are the ornaments of timeless beauty.

She takes a sip of her red wine. Her lips are blasted with color and taste. She moves elegantly throughout the kitchen. She dances to her own tune—a tune so beautiful it could rival the best orchestras in the world. She dances as if no one is watching.

I am her only audience. I am the sole ticket holder of this amazing performance as I watch her display a spectacle that is truly spellbinding.

She garnishes the plates, pours another glass of wine, and looks over at me.

"Dinner is ready."

As I continue to look at her, she is an image of utter immaculateness. She walks over to me. My breathing slows, my heart slows, and even the ticks of time come to a stop.

I can't breathe since I am not used to a love like this.

She kisses me, and once she does, I feel life breathed into me. She pulls back, and I am in complete awe, for I have never felt a love so powerful.

She looks at me.

"Are you okay?"

I try to find the words, but I'm robbed of them. Instead, I place my hands on her immaculate face. I gaze into the soul of her eyes and kiss her like never before.

This is true love. This is what I have always wanted my entire life.

# Conflict

I am walking around my office, listening to our quarterly report about BlackStone. I know that Sky is somewhere in the house, near to me, but my senses look for and crave her at all times. I feel like I'm a caged lion waiting to break free from this prison.

I try to focus. I try to commit to where I know I should be. Three, two, one, commit. I listen to what is being said.

"We delivered again with another great quarter. Revenues continue to climb as the business sides continue to grow. Total revenue grew 6.1% and increased 8% for the year. Our U.S. subsidiaries grew over 36%, while our international sales grew 55%. Because of this, we are expecting to hire an additional 225,000 employees worldwide in the next few quarters. Due to our international portfolio last year, we took some decisive action since we have strong momentum going forward. Our plants in Chile…"

As soon as I try to commit to the biggest conglomerate in the world, which I built from the bottom up, I feel that it's slipping away to a far distant echo that I can no longer focus on. My mind goes to where it knows my home is: her face, her touch, and that small curl in her lip when she smiles at me.

My universe is speaking to me right now. I do not see her, and yet I can hear her thoughts, her blood pumping, and the magnificent sound of her heart as it beats in synch with mine.

She is like a drug. I need to smell her. Feel the constant touch of her body up against mine. The sound of her slowly kissing my lips, the stroke of her hand behind the back of my head, and the soft smile she always gives me.

I need to focus. I must take care of what is now taking care of us for the rest of our lives. I wipe my forehead in frustration. Nia catches me as she is listening in and watching my reaction to what is being said. She pauses the conference and asks if I am okay.

I lie so that she won't know my real pain. Nia is smart. I must play this tactfully and return to my company. I tell her that I'm fine, that the small print is giving me a headache. She immediately calls for someone to send the report to me again, but with a larger print.

I try to stop her, persuade her, but now I must fully commit to this lie. None of this would have happened if I had just focused on what's at hand.

I return, fully focused and committed. The conference continues after a few short seconds.

"Again, the company posted a quarterly record of $7.8 trillion, an all-time record quarterly earnings per diluted share of $6.78 a share.."

The battle continues as Sky uses her power of love to speak to my soul. I can hear her calling my name so loudly that it rearranges the heavens. This power latches on to my soul and does not let go. I get up and excuse myself from the conference call.

I begin my search for Sky, for my universe. She calls for me yet again. My soul aches for her touch. The sound of her heartbeat grows louder as I am nearing her. I go deep into the cellar, for I know she is there.

As I go deeper, I see her. She is holding a bottle of wine. She looks up at me and is startled.

"Ian, I was just thinking of you."

I say nothing to her. I grab the bottle of wine and place it to the side. We are surrounded by some of the best wines in the world—many aged over several decades, and many aged for over a century.

Time plays a vital role in the maturity of the wine. Right now, I don't have the time or the disposition to wait on what is already waiting for me. I grab her and pull her into me. Immediately, my soul is at rest. I kiss her and embrace her with everything I have. I look down at her.

"Till the sun dies."

# My Universe

The snow falls outside our house in Montana. I'm here to oversee a project that has started construction but is rapidly moving ahead of schedule. It is a project solely made for her, and in time, for others. But for now, it is being built for her.

Ice crystals form all around the house, and the windows have a light haze around them. The cold bites hard if journeyed into, but she sits by the fireplace, reading her book. One of her lazy afternoon delights.

She is coiled in a blanket and protected from the elements outside. Never will she know an element that will try to harm her, for it is my responsibility and my undying love to protect her from everything and anything.

I place a cup of tea next to my Queen.

"Thank you."

I lean in and kiss her.

"I love you."

"I love you, too."

I place another log in the fireplace. The log crackles softly.

I lie on the other end of the couch, grab my book, and begin to read. I feel the blanket being moved, and before I know it, my universe is underneath my arms.

"You are so warm," she says. "I love it that you are always warm."

I kiss the top of her head and begin to run my fingers slowly through her hair. My entire universe is coiled next to me. As I touch her hair, I look at this woman, and I cannot imagine a life without her. For so long, I thought love was nonexistent. For so long, I accepted that love wasn't meant for me. And for so long, I was proven correct. That is until Sky came along.

She proved everything wrong when I was trying so hard to prove it right. She is my universe. She is my reason and my purpose in life. I would rather die than lose her. I want to hold her until the end of time. And even then, time will have to fight me for her.

She looks up at me.

"Are you okay?"

I touch the side of her face and look into her world of blue.

"I'm okay. I'm more than okay."

She places her hand behind my head and pulls me into her. Her kiss is majestic. It is life, and my universe chooses to only give it to me.

# Garden

*Although you are my angel, you can turn to your fierce and wicked side. You are pleasurable. Your body is beyond words. Your eyes look deep into my soul. You search deeper until you find what you are looking for.*

*Calmness comes over me. Quietness is spread throughout my body.*

*I feel safe with you, and that is your intention all along.*

*With my guard down, you unleash your savagery upon me. Rather than run away, I run to you, not fearing what you will do to me.*

*I love your dominance and the love you bring with your domination. You are my sinful apple that has fallen from the tree, and I cannot wait to bite into you.*

*I want to ravage you like a predator that devours its prey.*

*I want to unleash my devastating storm upon you. The kind that strips Mother Nature of her skin and kills without a conscience.*

*This is what you bring out of me, a carnal side that only you can handle and that only you can match.*

*My beautiful angel from above, spread your legs across the heavens and invite me into your garden.*

# North Star

The hull of the boat divides the water beneath us. She is a beauty in the seas but a beast once given full throttle. I guide her gently in the light of the moon. My North Star stands at the bow of the boat.

She is radiant as her hair touches the outer edges of the moon. She tosses her hair to one side, and the beautiful flowing hair now dips into the horizon of the water.

No need to look above for answers or directions. No need to look at maps or compasses. My North Star guides me through these waters, which can be the calmest ever known or the most violent ever seen.

Tonight, the sea lies calmly to give a wide birth to my universe, my North Star.

She turns to me, and in the darkness, her blue eyes glow in the night. I look into her eyes and wonder what could be more beautiful and calming to the senses.

I leave the steering wheel and let the sea take us where she may. I walk out to her, my North Star. Her hair is flowing across the night skies. She reaches for me, I grab her hand. She steps forward and places one hand on my face.

I feel the electrical surge come across my body. I place my hand across her cheek and run my finger across her warm-blooded lips. She closes her eyes, relaxes, and leans into my touch.

Again, I feel her powerful love. Time begins to slow. The waters no longer flow. The clouds no longer roam the skies. The stars in the heavens no longer flicker.

I feel my heartbeat begin to slow. I look at her as she stands before me with her eyes still closed and her lips of wonder waiting for me. I lean in and kiss her lush, flowing lips.

Life once again is breathed into me and into the world around us. I hear the waters begin to flow, the clouds pass, the moon and the heavens begin to sparkle once more.

I look down at Sky, and I am in complete wonder of her and this powerful love.

The North Star guides us through the night—my North Star, that is.

# Lion Versus Lamb

The water trickles at first and then begins to pour down like a thunderstorm. Enclosing the water is a see-through glass from all sides. Sky enters the transparent enclosure. She walks underneath the thunderstorm of water from above.

She embraces the free-flowing water as it runs down her naked body. The speed of the water increases as it travels down her curvaceous figure. She is smooth, fast, and slick. Not even the water can handle her curves as it drips from all angles.

She raises her head, allowing the water to run down her beautiful face. Poseidon, the God of the sea, could not create such a majestic waterfall if he had tried.

I walk in and give the command for the lights to be turned off. Immediately, the water turns a luminous blue as it rushes down her body. When she opens her eyes, darkness surrounds her.

She gives the command for the lights to come on. But Gesture senses my presence and will not allow it. From the darkness, a spec of light will be given, all that I will allow. In the shadows, she can see me flowing in and out of the darkness.

Like a lion, I am circling my sacrificial lamb. She follows me as I continue to circle her. With each turn, a piece of clothing falls from my body.

Soon, only a piece of glass separates us. She steps back, the sensual side of her begging for me to come inside her enclosure. She continues to let the water rush down her uncontrollable curves.

I open the glass door and walk towards her. I stand beneath the water with her. I run my hands up her face and to the back of her head. I pause.

She looks at me.

"Tell me."

I grab a handful of her hair and gently squeeze it. As she closes her eyes, a small breath of pleasure and pain escapes her.

"Who do you belong to?" I whisper.

She looks deep into my soul, smiles, jumps ever so gracefully, and wraps her precious yet powerful legs around my waist. She again looks deep into my eyes.

"No, who do *you* belong to?" she says.

I run my hands down her back and cradle my benevolence.

"You, my love. Only you."

The tables have turned. I walked in as the dominant one, only to be dominated by this creature who can have me anytime she wants.

I press her up against the glass and enter her, but only because the lioness allows it.

# The Storm

The house is on the highest part of the Colorado Rockies. I stand looking out the clear thirty-three-foot solid window pane. I wave my hand across the pane, which slides open gracefully. I walk out to the balcony and stare at the beautiful heavens.

I raise my glass with the finest of Scotch, a Macallan 64-year-old, and toast it to the sky. It is out of respect that I only drink the finest to the many beautiful stars above.

I look at my watch. She's running late yet again. Even at her worst, she is a sight to look at it, but when she dresses up, she is nothing short of absolute perfection.

The floor gently shakes as I see a flash of lightning in the distance. A storm is rapidly approaching.

As I turn around, the glass door has silently closed. On the other side, I see a woman with undeniable force and beauty.

She is wearing a tightly fitted black dress, my favorite color. The temptress teases me as she runs her finger across her lower lip. Her eyes tell me that she is to be treated like a Queen, and yet, a darker side of her begins to emerge.

She takes off her high heels and steps back as she scans me from top to bottom.

I know this game. I know this game very well. I put the Scotch on the floor. It isn't a piece of clothing, but it still belongs to me.

She smiles in a way that tells me it is time to play. She reaches behind her neck, unclasps her necklace, and lays it to the side.

I undo my watch and likewise put it to the side.

She takes off one earring.

I take off my coat.

She takes off her other earring.

I take off my jacket.

She takes off her platinum bracelet.

I take off my shoes and socks, and she follows with two more bracelets and two rings.

She hikes the tiny black dress up a little, reaches underneath, pulls down her panties, and holds them in one hand.

I take off my pants and drop them to the side.

She smiles and begins to touch her bottom lip once again, but this time more sensually. She takes one step back.

My reaction is instant as my happiness changes to confusion.

She looks at my shirt with an aroused smile.

I take off one cufflink, and she takes one more step back.

I am about to take a step forward when she shakes her head and threatens to take another step back.

She looks at the other cufflink and nods to it. She is altering the rules, but I am all too happy to indulge her.

The storm is approaching, and I feel the first drop of rain on my face. I turn away as the orchestra of lightning strikes and thunder approaches. I turn back to her and begin to unbutton my shirt.

She bites her lower lip as I put my shirt aside.

She takes one step forward.

The rain begins to pour, but I do not break eye contact with her. I slide off my briefs and stand naked before her.

The lightning produces a magnificent show. The thunder shakes the floors beneath us.

She takes another step forward, then waves her hand across the window pane and enters my world of beauty and power.

The thunder cracks with each step she takes toward me.

She takes off her dress and is finally exposed to me and the storm.

The raincoats her entire body with liquid diamonds as if she were the goddess of the storm.

I stand over my luminescent goddess.

Placing her hands on my chest, she says, "Take me!"

I pick her up and wrap her legs around me.

I enter her moist Amazon.

She raises her head and stares at the thunderstorm above.

I press my head into her breasts and become one with my goddess.

# Masterpiece

We walk in as strangers, barely even noticing each other. We wander around the great halls of the museum, admiring the fine works of art, but we never lose sight of each other.

She gently looks over her shoulder to see if I am still behind her.

She smiles and continues to roam the great halls. She stops to admire a painting, but it's her way of letting me get closer to her.

I see how she appreciates the fine works of art that surround us, but the only fine work that I can and will appreciate is hers. She will never leave my sight, for I will never allow it. I regard her as the greatest masterpiece that time has ever created.

I move silently and cautiously among the passersby, disappearing from her line of sight. I watch from a secluded corner as she tries to find me.

Her hair whips in panic as she turns in every direction. Her eyes search for me while her hands pray that she has not lost me.

I am tormented to see her in such pain.

I rejoin her world, in which everything is just the two of us.

Again, I move through the crowd, never losing sight of my universe.

I am closer to my Queen. I am closer to making this kingdom great once again. I am within arm's reach now, yet she is still searching for me.

I walk past her, and with a gentle touch, I rub my hand against her face.

She feels my touch, and her reaction is swift, but I have already left her. I see her searching again till she finally sees me standing in a crowd. She smiles and walks toward me.

As she comes near, she holds out her hand.

I grab it, and we are whole once more. We roam the great halls together. This time, we never break from each other.

We leave the museum, but we are different now. We came in as strangers… We leave as husband and wife.

# The Bath

I miss her so much as the plane cuts the night like a knife. But it's not fast enough to get to her. I hate being away from her. As I look out the window, I wonder what she's doing. I'm only a few hours away from her, but it feels like a world away from the universe that I love and desire.

As I close my eyes, I fill my head with the thoughts and memories of my love. I can feel her touch. I feel my heart pumping faster when she calls my name. The smile she gives me is like a miracle of life bestowed on me.

Her being alone without me by her side troubles me greatly. I am protective of her; I would gladly stand in harm's way for her. She is my wife, my love, and my best friend. Who better to protect with all that I have when it comes to my universe?

She once told me that she read of a woman who told her lover, "Till the moon turns to rust, I will love you." She looked into my eyes and told me that her love would not only rival that but exceed it.

Only once in a lifetime does one come across a woman who willingly and utterly expresses herself in such a way. I am so lucky to experience that type of love and devotion.

As I look out the window, I can't wait to get to my wife. I have waited forever and a day to have a kingdom like this. When I see her, I proudly call her my Queen. I proudly take her hand into mine and show her that she is like no other.

When the plane lands, I would jump out the window if I could. My passion for her is so great that I would do so. When the hatch opens, I cannot walk down the ramp fast enough. I quickly get into the car waiting for me.

While I am closer to her, she is still a world away. I miss her and need her in my arms. My patience wears thin, and my conscience runs wild as I tremble to be in her presence. I am only a few miles away from her, but I might as well be a world away.

The car pulls up to our house. I do not wait for my door to be opened. I immediately jump out of the car while it is still rolling.

When Gesture opens the front door for me, I know that Sky is aware that I am home. But that is not enough because I still cannot see her or hold her.

Our love is so strong that I know exactly where she is as I walk through the house, wishing it were smaller.

*God, do I miss her!*

I finally come to where she is and slowly open the bathroom door. She is lying in a tub of bubbles, with lit candles and an aroma that fills the room with pure delight.

Turning to me with a smile, she says, "My love!"

Her words penetrate my body and soul. I walk over to the tub and look down at her.

"Are you okay?" she asks.

I say nothing because I am not okay. As I look into her eyes, they hold my universe. I have been away far too long.

I am wearing a five-thousand-dollar suit, but that does not stop me from getting into the tub with her. She looks at me with astonishment. I just look at this woman that I love so much. My love is so great that I want to shed tears for her because she is finally within my reach.

I come closer to her, raise my hand through the water, and touch her face.

"Ian, are you okay?" she asks again.

I raise my other hand to touch the other side of her face.

I lean in and kiss the lips of life.

I feel my body come alive. My skin breathes in her aroma. My heart skips a beat or two. I savor the taste of her lips. I open my eyes. I look at my beautiful wife.

"Mine," I whisper.

"Always," she says softly.

She smiles as she wraps her arms around me and gives me a kiss that could last a lifetime.

I am finally in her world, in her universe, and I wouldn't want to be anywhere else.

# A New Year

The evening is set perfectly. We are among friends from San Antonio, whose streets are lined with happiness. As before and always, we are both sought after and occasionally separated, but my eyes always search for her.

I am happy to be among so many friends who are like family to me, and they have taken Sky in as one of their own. She is hugged and kissed countless times, and I feel comfortable that she is among so many great people who have been in my life for so long.

I feel a tap on my shoulder, turn around, and next to me is the most powerful woman in the business world, Nia, my one-time assistant and now the CEO of my company, BlackStone. I immediately hug her and kiss her on her cheek.

"How are you doing, Nia?"

"Busy, but that's always going to be the case with BlackStone. How is Sky? I haven't seen her tonight."

I turn around and search for the tiara that I asked her to wear and immediately spot her. I lean back and point out to Nia where she is. Nia looks at Sky for a moment.

"She's lovely as always, Ian."

"Yes, she is. Isn't she?"

A loud voice shouts, "One minute left till the New Year."

I turn to Nia, who has a smile on her face.

"Go to her, Ian," she says.

I nod my head, embrace my friend and mentor, and wish her a Happy New Year. She kisses me on the cheek and wishes me the same.

I begin walking toward Sky as the ball on top of the Tower of America has begun its descent for the final minute. My journey to her becomes more difficult when I am stopped several times and wished a Happy New Year.

My view of Sky is lost as so many people converge on one another to share this moment. I do my best to be nice by hugging and kissing those who wish me a Happy New Year, but the only person I want to hold this night is her.

The ball is in its final seconds. She turns and looks for me but cannot see me.

Four seconds….

Three seconds….

The crowd goes into a frenzy as the last seconds are about to tick away. I feel as if time is standing still and waiting for me to get to her. I move through the crowd effortlessly and am finally in her presence.

Two seconds….

I grab her waist and turn her to me. I look into her eyes and show her all the love I have for her. I show her a world in which I could not exist without her. I show her a world that only she inhabits.

One second….

I lean in to kiss the most beautiful woman who has ever graced my eyes and who has ever walked the face of the Earth. I hold her tight and dearly to me.

Fireworks go off in every direction; confetti is falling all over us. Cheers and laughter surround us, but right now, this moment can only belong to her.

Happy New Year, my love!

# A Day of Hearts

We are in one of the most secluded parts of New Zealand. The waves crash onto the cliff below the house. Over the horizon, dawn is beginning to break. I turn to my universe as she enjoys her slumber.

I step out onto the balcony to grab my spear gun.

I look out over the cliff at the calm blue water of the Pacific. The snowcapped mountains in the distance are the only friends that surround us.

The first hints of a new day begin as the rays of the sun make their way toward us.

The sun's rays finally reach us and engulf our room with sunlight. I turn around, and even in rest, Sky's beauty and splendor are unrivaled.

"Infinite black," I tell Gesture.

Immediately, the windows turn from clear to solid pitch-black. Sky is not to be disturbed as I make her morning breakfast.

Looking down at my daughter, I say, "Take care of Sky, Mena. I'll be right back."

I take in a deep breath and begin my run. As I do, I pick up momentum. I am fast, I am alive with passion, and I am filled with love and devotion.

I am nearing the edge of the cliff with the wind to my back. I must launch with no hesitation and no fear. I see the end. I gather my composure, launch myself from the cliff, and dive sixty-three feet into the Pacific Ocean.

I am back on land, carrying four lobsters and one snapper that weighs at least fifteen pounds. I make my way to the outdoor kitchen and lay everything on the cutting board.

I clean all of my catch and then begin to cook. I start with the lobster omelet. I mix the lobster together with chili, spring onion, and some ponzu sauce. I thoroughly wash the snapper again and filet it, season it with salt and pepper, add some rosemary and lemon, and throw it in the oven.

My universe is still asleep. I ask Gesture to peel back the darkness and allow the day to start for my love. The sun enters the room and shines upon her.

I look down at Mena.

"Go give your mother a kiss good morning."

Mena jumps on the bed and begins to softly lick Sky's face. My universe begins to awaken. She squints and smiles as she immediately hugs Mena's fur coat.

"What are you doing up so early?" she asks.

I come from around the bed.

"Happy Valentine's Day!"

From behind my back, I extend a single red rose to her.

"Oh, baby!" she says with excitement. "Happy Valentine's Day to you, too!"

I lean over to kiss her on the side of the cheek. I grab her hand and take her outside, where her morning breakfast is waiting for her. The table is set overlooking the ocean. I pull her chair out and seat her.

She stares at the food with wonder. Looking up at me, she says, "This looks amazing!"

I smile and nod at the compliment. Mena is beginning to lick her chops.

"I didn't forget about you, girl," I say, placing her plate on the floor.

Then I sit down next to my universe, lean over, and kiss her once again.

"Eat, my love."

I look down at Mena.

"Eat, baby."

The two of them begin to eat. While I myself am starving, I can't help taking a few moments to enjoy the view of my girls eating and relaxing on the gorgeous day of hearts.

# No Ordinary Love

I fold the napkin and place it on my plate. My palate is satisfied beyond measure, and yet I am starving—not for food, but for her—her intellect, vigor, passion, and way of seeing things.

My appetite can only be filled by the deep conversations that she brings. Her mind can never be measured. When she talks to me, I can hear the depth of her intelligence. I give her my undivided attention as I listen to an angel preaching words that many would follow.

I have spoken to four presidents, five Nobel Peace Prize winners, countless prime ministers, and two popes, but none could rival her passion. I may be biased, but so what if I am? She is my friend, my best friend, and my most trusted individual through space and time. But above all else, she is my wife.

My only regret is that I didn't meet her sooner. If I had, God help those who stood in my way. But maybe that is the trade-off. I might have been a tyrant of old, conquering all lands, but instead, I am a tyrant of a different sort, a tyrant of compassion and understanding—if there is such a thing.

She has my ears, eyes, thoughts, and undying love for her. I listen to all that she has to say. As I stare at her, I cannot measure how much love I have for this woman.

I put up my hand to ask her to pause for that one second it will take me to walk over to her. I kneel beside her and look into her blue eyes.

She tilts her head slightly to one side, looking deep into my eyes.

Smiling, she says, "Ian, what is it?"

I love it when she says my name. I could listen to her say my name for all eternity. She is my island of hope.

I place my hands on her face. She closes her eyes as she gently leans into my warm touch. When she opens her eyes, I show her the calm she seeks in this world.

I lean in to kiss her lips, which taste like fine vintage wine. But she is far from vintage. She is the new world I have been waiting for my whole life. We embrace our world, showing that we share the same breath, the same air of life.

I open my eyes. She is frozen in time.

Then, suddenly, she is alive as life is breathed into her.

She opens her eyes.

"How do you do that?" she asks. "How do you make me feel a love greater than before?"

"It was always there, my love. It was you who held the key for it to be unlocked. It was you who showed me the depths of love, and it is you who will continue to show me."

A small tear begins to form at the corner of her right eye. I stop it from running down her immaculate face.

"I love you, Ian," she whispers.

"I love you, Sky. I have loved you since the beginning of time."

# A Rough Day

I lie in bed with a book, a real book. I can still feel the words and smell the paper they are printed on. I read the words of a book that is exceptionally well-written and extremely intelligent. It is a submission from a young man who has incredible talent.

As I continue to read the book, Gesture announces that Sky is home. She had been away at meetings all day, working for her charitable organizations.

I continue to read the book. The words are flawless and brilliant, and the content is tremendous. I turn to the front cover to learn the author's name. As I do, the bedroom door slides open.

Even after twelve hours of being away all day, she is more beautiful than she was this morning. She smiles at me, sending indescribable warmth through me.

Her walk toward me is slow. Her face shows the long hours she has put in. She lets her hair down, which falls like a majestic cascade of liquid gold. When her eyes engulf me, I am hypnotized by this woman. I can smell her fragrance from across the room.

The sun-rich jasmine and juniper flow from her with honeydew nectar and a touch of rose, leaving a trail of scent behind her.

I am frozen. I am so unable to handle her natural beauty that I forget how to breathe, and my heart begins to slow.

She bends over. The magnificent waterfall of her golden hair drapes across my chest. She leans in to give me a kiss.

I taste my apple, which is beyond sweet. She gives the kiss of life to me. My heart begins to beat with hers as air fills my lungs.

She does not stop with a kiss but slowly hikes up her skirt and climbs on top of me. Her sensual smile once again sends a feeling through me that eagerly awaits her next touch.

She leans in more, kisses my neck, and rubs her face against mine. She places her hands on my face and breathes me in.

I open myself to her and allow my soul to be touched by her.

She caresses, warms, and invigorates my soul.

Her eyes are closed as she raises herself. She moves her head around slowly as she lets out a small sigh. She slowly uses one hand to undo the first two buttons of her blouse.

When she does, I see that she has no visible gap between her breasts. She is full and plentiful. Her cleavage is irrefutably the best I have ever seen.

But her world of wonder does not stop there. She opens her eyes and stares into the depths of my soul. Her sensual side has turned into carnage.

I know what it is she seeks. I willingly give myself to her so that she may feed.

She reaches down between her legs and finds that I am fully aroused as I wait to enter her garden.

She licks her lips as she firmly grabs what is hers and only hers.

I feel the stroke of her hand as I pulsate vigorously with each stroke.

She calls the beast from within. He is ready to break the cage and devour this woman, but I do not set him free—not yet.

She slowly guides me into her garden, losing her breath as her sensual juices run down me.

As I grab her waist, I can feel her strength squeezing me from within.

Not yet…. Not yet.

It is she who must feed first until she is fully satisfied. She always pushes me to the brink, but I always wait until she is pleased, no matter how much time she takes and no matter how much she wants to be pleased.

When her appetite has been gratified, she looks at me with such pleasure and then allows me to feed. I finally unleash the beast from within.

I transform into what she has beckoned.

I lie on top of her. She opens herself to me, allowing me to feast on her soul. Her garden is spread wider as I go deeper. I feel, search, and fill every inch of her garden.

She tries to contain the beast, but she finds herself asking for it to tear into her.

As I unleash what she asks for, a torrent of rain pours into her garden.

When I pull back the beast, I immediately check to see if my Queen is alright.

She wipes away the perspiration on my forehead, then smiles, kisses me, and holds me close to her.

I can feel her heartbeat.

I can feel her breath.

I can feel her love.

I can feel my universe.

# A Nightmare

No matter how much I hold on to her hand, she is being pulled away from me. The moment our fingertips no longer touch, I fight with all that I have to get to her. My breathing is labored, my legs hurt, and my heart is pounding out of my chest.

I still see a vision of her, but as suddenly as she is there, she is gone from sight. I chase her in the darkness, never wanting to give up until I can hold her once again. Without warning, I begin to fall into the depths of a black abyss.

I hear a faint voice. Looking up, I see her spinning in midair. She spins around and around, never coming toward me. From the darkness, a hand comes toward me from the side. I look up, and I see a hand grab her hand.

I immediately climb this black abyss, but then, from the depths, another hand grabs my foot. The grasp is too weak, and I am too strong to be denied.

A third hand appears and grabs my other foot.

I am not to be denied as I continue my climb toward her. Another hand, followed by another, and another, and another, till finally, a hand reaches across my eyes. Its grasp begins to tighten. I am squeezed with such force that it hurts to breathe.

The hands take my eyes, which I have always said belong entirely to her. I grow weaker, my heart begins to slow. The light from within me begins to flicker.

From a distance, I hear an angelic voice, a voice so strong that the flame from within is ignited with passion and love.

I have yet to enjoy my finest hour. Let this be the time that I do. I begin to pry off the hands of solitude and darkness. They come back with more hands, and yet I grow stronger. My strength is a match they can no longer contain.

The distance is great, but I push my heart, body, and soul toward her. I hear her voice again, which only propels me faster.

I feel a hand brush across my chest, but this touch is different. This touch is hers.

You call out my name again, and in the distance, a tiny speck of light begins to show itself to me. I slowly open my eyes. You are sitting on the bed, touching my chest.

"My love," she says, "are you alright?"

She is an angel who has rescued me once again. I look deep into her eyes. I softly touch the bottom of her chin. Again, she asks if I am alright, but the truth is, I am not. I know that there will be a time when one of us will have to leave, but it won't be tonight.

"I'm fine," I say with a smile, raising my arm so that she can come and lie next to me. As she lays her head on my chest, the universe is made right again. We fall asleep, never letting anything disrupt us.

# A Walk in the Clouds

I feel the rays of the sun gently warm my skin. I open my eyes and reach for her, but her side of the bed is cold. I lift myself from the bed and search for her. I go from room to room, finally coming to the balcony. I see her walking among the clouds. Her white robe blends in with them as if she is walking on air.

She has dreamt about coming to Japan and taking a walk in the clouds. She walks ever so gracefully as she is living one of her dreams. She turns and sees me, gesturing for me to come to her.

I cannot see the floor beneath me. All I know is that I am several thousand feet in the air with this beautiful woman. I take my first steps toward my Queen.

The sun is only an arm's length away from her. She stands above the world in the most magnificent way possible. She moves slowly as her fingertips graze the tops of the clouds.

She takes in a deep breath and closes her eyes. The rays of the sun caress her face.

I come from behind her and draw her into me. She willingly gives into my embrace. She turns around and looks up into my eyes.

Without words, she says everything she is feeling. She tells me that she loves me. She tells me that she is the happiest woman on this Earth. She tells me that she would never leave my side. She tells me that she couldn't be any happier. And lastly, she tells me that she is proud to be my wife.

I look at this woman, who only a year ago was a stranger and now is the cornerstone of my heart and soul. I softly touch her lips and the side of her face.

"I know," I say. "We are not two separate beats; we are but a single beat."

I kiss her, and we hold on to each other passionately as husband and wife above the clouds.

# The Art of Love

I arrive at an abandoned warehouse. There is nothing around for miles. When I walk into the rust-covered building, large flowing white sheets are hanging from the rafters, which come down to the floor. A solid white sheet, eight feet tall, runs the length of the back wall and the floor.

Black, gold, and red paint cans are on the floor with brushes. I hear a noise and search through the white sheets. I see my angel. When the wind blows the sheets, it hides her from me completely.

She reappears. Her hair is wet and brushed back. She is wearing a see-through white dress with open sides. As she walks toward me, she is breathtaking. She says nothing as she grabs my hand and guides me through the maze of white sheets.

When we come to the paint and the brushes, she turns around and smiles. Still, she says nothing. She begins to undress me till I am naked to only her and the rustic warehouse. As she slides the dress off her shoulders, it falls to the floor.

I look at every inch of her, but the most beautiful part of her is her love for me. She grabs a paintbrush, dips it into the black paint, and begins to paint my chest. I grab a brush, dip it into the bright red paint, and begin to paint her shoulders.

I paint her legs gold because legs like hers are meant to be dipped in gold. I take my time as I paint every inch of her legs. The bristles of the brush show how curvy she is. Wet paint drips from her thigh. I am mesmerized by the sight.

Soon, we are a mixture of gold, black, and red paint. She walks over to the long white sheet on the wall, turns around, looks at me, and slowly places her mosaic body against the sheet. As she steps forward, the beautiful imprint of her body is immaculate.

I walk up to her and run my fingers down the side of her face. She looks into my eyes.

"Paint the walls with me," she says.

I back her up against the wall, raise her hands above her head, and run my hand down her face, down her breasts, and past her stomach. She is wet and full of anticipation.

Hours later, the sun begins its retreat behind the horizon. We sit together. She leans back and rests her head on my chest.

"What do you think?" she asks.

I look at the sheet and see the lovemaking of a man and a woman who define the words *love* and *devotion*.

"Magnificent," I say.

# Burning Man

The desert is harsh as the winds gust, and the sandstorms cover the senses. Yet, many flock to the man-made city in the desert, wearing the most art-decorated costumes and leaving little to the imagination as self-expression of the human body is exposed in many forms.

I have traveled the world and seen many cultures, but nothing quite like this. It is a throwback time, yet the most modern of young minds bring the spectacle of life to another form. There is no judgment here, there is no commerce, and love is in abundance.

While I could have brought everything to make the desert into a five-star hotel, she did not allow it. We bought an old beat-up Chevy Blazer and loaded it with chairs, food, water, toiletries, two bikes, and a tent with three separate rooms. In the back seat, with not very much room, was Mena—her tail wagging and her black tongue hanging out as she knew she was on another adventure with mom and dad.

Eight hundred dollars in cash is what I had, and it is what I gave at the gate for us to become burners. The rest would be what Sky called gifting. The value of a gift is unconditional. Gifting does not contemplate a return or an exchange for something of equal value— a simple motto, but something that opened my eyes about humanity still caring for one another. Everything that we brought was gifted, including the tent, in which people could stay for free.

I sit on the lawn chair with Mena by my side and watch as Sky hands out fruit and water to anybody who walks by our camp. Many do, and many call our camp home.

A hug and a smile are all Sky asks if they decide to stay. Every one of them is so grateful that the hugs and kisses last an eternity. It is like watching her motherly instinct kick into high gear. She accepts all and turns away none.

Our camp grows until the last night when a DJ whom we had put up for the night asks if he can DJ at our camp. We accept his gift, and the turnout is more than we anticipated. The light show above our heads is spectacular. Sky dances under the lights as the music unleashes her free spirit.

Mena and I watch this woman who owns every part of us and depends on her for every single breath this life gives us. As I watch my universe, I am completely lost in her natural beauty and in her blue cosmos.

I suddenly feel a tap on my shoulder. It is an old man in his eighties, possibly older.

"Yes, sir?"

"How are you, young man? Is that chair taken?"

"No, please feel free to have a seat. Would you like a bottle of water as well?"

"No, thank you, young man. I just need to take a quick break."

He strolls past me. He is wearing a white t-shirt with denim overalls, knee-high socks, white sneakers, and a cowboy hat. He pauses, smiles, and gently pets the top of Mena's head. She approves with the wag of her tail.

I look out over the crowd, but my eyes effortlessly find their way back to Sky. I once again find myself lost in her beauty. As I am completely focused on her, I hear the old man speak to me.

"How I wish I still had my old lady around to look at her the way you look at your wife!"

"Oh, thank you, but I am sorry for your loss. My condolences."

He tips his hat toward me.

"How long have you two been married?"

"Almost a year."

"Oh, you are still in your honeymoon phase. I remember those times and look back at them as the greatest moments I ever loved someone."

"How long were you married, if you don't mind my asking?"

"Eighty-one glorious years. But they still weren't enough to show her how much I truly loved her before she passed away."

I am astonished to hear how long he was married.

"I'm sorry, sir," I say. "But how old are you?"

"I am ninety-eight years old. We got married when we were sixteen. Just a couple of young dumb kids who were in love and thought we could rule the world."

"Wait! If you're ninety-eight, that means she passed away last year?"

"Today is the day I lost her last year."

"Oh, I'm so sorry. I truly am."

He smiles.

"Don't be. I've been looking forward to this day for a whole year, and I'm finally happy it's here."

Intrigued by his response, I ask him why. He begins to explain that he has traveled around the whole world during the past year. He visited the plains of Africa, the misty waterfalls of Costa Rica, the icy underground caves of Iceland, the towering mountains of New Zealand, the crystal clear waters of the Dominican Republic, the northern lights of Norway, the powdery ski slopes of Switzerland, the snowcapped volcanoes of Mexico, and many other places, with Burning Man as his last stop.

He then describes the night his wife died. She told him to travel the world, to do what they had promised they would do together, but they never could since life brought them many kids, along with many grandchildren, great-grandchildren, and even great-great-grandchildren.

She told him that she would be there with him wherever he traveled but that for exactly one year, she would be calling him home to her.

As I listen to his incredible story, words escape me. I am overflowing with emotions for a stranger I hardly know.

"Sir, I don't know what to say."

He smiles as he struggles to get up from his chair.

I immediately get up from mine to assist the old man.

"Sir, you don't have to leave. You are more than welcome to stay as long as you like. We have rooms in the tent you can stay in."

He looks right at me.

"You're a good man with a good heart," he says. "But it's time for me to leave."

"Can I get you anything? Anything at all?"

He gently pats the side of my face.

"I'm good, thank you."

He slowly begins to walk away.

I can't let him leave. Not without asking. I quickly walk over to him.

"Sir?"

He slowly turns around.

"Yes, son?"

"I sometimes fear that I won't have a love like that, that I'm not showing or giving enough to her. How did you do it?"

His eyes light up as a smile comes across him as if life is instilled in him once again. He places his hand on my shoulder.

"Marry her. Marry her every day of your life. Tell her 'I do' every single day of your life. And look at her as if it's the first time you have ever laid eyes on her."

Without saying anything else, he walks away into the night.

I watch as the old man strolls away. I have never had a male role model to look up to, but in the few minutes I have come to know this old man, I can honestly say that he is my role model and mentor.

I walk through the crowds, looking for Sky. As soon as I see her, I walk up to her. She is sweaty from all the dancing, but that does not stop me from holding on to this beautiful woman. I look into her eyes

The music begins to fade. The crowd begins to disappear into the background.

"Will you marry me?" I say softly.

"What?"

"Will you marry me?"

"Ian, we're already married."

I gently push back a string of her hair behind her ear.

"Will you marry me?"

She slightly tilts her head to one side.

"Baby, what's wrong?" she asks, looking concerned.

"Nothing. Will you marry me?"

She smiles.

"Yes, my love, I will marry you."

I smile because it feels like this is the first time I'm asking for her hand in marriage, and it feels like it's the first time I'm hearing her say "Yes."

I stare at my beautiful wife as I always do as if it's the first time she has captured my eyes. But she has captured more than that. She has captured me until the end of time and my undying love for her.

I gently bring her into me and seal our love with an eternal kiss under the night skies of the Burning Man.

# A Talk Among Best of Friends

We are at the Rock, our private island near Spain. It is another banner quarter for BlackRock, and I have flown in most of the company to celebrate. I sit at the top of the stairs with Mena by my side, watching the party below.

I brush Mena's head softly.

She looks at me with her purple tongue slightly hanging from her mouth.

"What is it, girl?"

She looks at the party below. I watch as her eyes follow Sky. She sticks her tongue back in when she sees another woman hugging Sky.

"Hey, she's okay," I say. "She's among family, remember? You can let your guard down for one night, girl."

Mena huffs.

"Alright. Alright, girl. But I understand. I wouldn't let my guard down, either. Look at her. She's perfect, she's humble, she's graceful, and she's absolutely beautiful."

I look at Mena and her stern posture.

"You know, girl, you've been a blessing to me as well. You literally came into my life when all that was ahead was a dark road. You made me come to feel again, to actually start to care for something in my life again. I owe you so much, and yet all you ask is to be by our side."

Mena continues staring at Sky and the people around her.

"Hey, you want to know something?" I say. "Did you know that your ancestors originally came from China?"

Mena looks at me.

"It's true. You're what were called the Chinese Guardian-Lion. It's very symbolic in that you are fiercely protective of your owners and property. As you should be, girl."

Mena turns her attention back to Sky. All I can do is smile as I continue to rub her soft coat.

"I know I haven't said it enough and tend to take for granted how much you love Sky and me, but I love you very much, Mena. *We* love you very much."

Mena slowly turns her head to look at me. Then, ever so softly, she licks the side of my face.

I smile.

"Shall we join the party?"

Her tail begins to wag.

"Very well, girl. Let's go say hi to the family."

# The Serenade

It is nearly 1:00 in the morning. We sit outside a restaurant called "La Hacienda." The trees are littered with small lights from within. Decorated lights stream across the outside patio and onto the outside bar, where the bartender looks on at the few patrons still drinking the cool night away.

A man in the corner of the restaurant is singing the last chord of a karaoke song.

Sky sits across from me, stirring her margarita. She wipes the rim of salt from the glass and licks it from her finger. Then she looks at me and smiles. As she peers into my soul, she goes into a trance.

I do not break from her stare. Instead, I invite her into my soul and let her search where she may.

She gets up and comes over to me. She leans over and acts as if she is going to give me a kiss but instead sits on my lap. She leans back into my body and grabs my hands, placing them on her thighs, my favorite parts of her body. I feel her curves as she presses my hands into her.

I can feel her breath on the side of my neck.

"This is for you, daddy."

She pushes herself off me and walks away, her black dress swaying from side to side. She pulls her hair out of the ponytail and lets it flow down her back the way I like it. She turns her face to me, but not all the way. She smiles and turns away.

She goes up to the mic. A small sigh comes from her. The song she chooses begins to play. She closes her eyes, and when she opens them again, she is in a different place as she begins to sing, "I've been drinking, I've been drinking...."

Her voice is soft, sultry, and seductive to the senses. Then it increases in volume as she sings directly to me. She moves like a serpent rising from a basket.

"Can't keep your eyes off my phatty daddy, I want you...."

She runs her hand down the middle of her breasts, down her stomach, to the side of her hip, and then flips her hair to one side.

"We be all night, love, love...."

Sky calls to me with her eyes, her body, and her heart.

I accept her invitation and walk slowly toward her. I stand in front of her, put my hand on her cheek, and follow it to her lips.

"Eat the cake, Anna Mae...."

She licks my finger without hesitation.

When the song is over, the few remaining patrons clap, as do the staff.

Sky looks at me while catching her breath.

"I want you, daddy."

"You will always have me, baby."

# Apple

The view is stunning as we stay on our secluded islands in the North Pacific Ocean. I watch from a distance as Sky slowly steps into the clearest waters in the world. Do my eyes deceive me? Is this goddess really walking on water?

Even with the beauty of the islands providing the backdrop, my universe robs them of my attention. I solely look at this woman as she makes her way to a waterfall. She turns, arches her back, and allows the water to christen her.

Her eyes are closed as Mother Nature embraces her with love and affection.

I don't know if there is enough time in this life to truly show her how much I love her. She gives me my strength and so much more.

In my life before her, I was allowing myself to starve into utter darkness, but she would not allow it as she pulled me from the edge. It's there that she nurtured me. I was thirsty, and she quenched my thirst.

She looked upon me with love and affection and not as a stranger. She broke me from my prison, clothed me, and helped me to fight this depression that I've had for so long.

I can no longer watch my apple. I must go to her.

I enter the water. The clarity is unlike anything I've ever seen, and I feel that I, too, am walking on water. I walk toward her as her eyes remain closed. Her beauty is so pleasing to my eyes that I cannot look away.

Her body is the definition of perfection. I admire all that is mine and all that she freely gives me. If this is our Eden, I would have to say that mankind is doomed again. I could not say no to this apple of my eye.

If we are truly born with sin, then why not indulge? The serpent would not have to entice me about this apple, for I would freely pick it.

I stand next to my obsession, my apple, my universe. I place both my hands on the side of her face. Instantly we are once again in synch as our beats become one.

I look into her eyes. I gently rub the tiny beads of water from her lips, for I am not thirsty for water but for her. I kiss her gently and passionately. The sound of the waterfall dissipates, the life from the island goes silent, and time begins to slow once more.

This is our Eden, and I will gladly pick the same fruit for all of eternity.

# 4:33 A.M.

Gesture rings the faint sound of a small chime to awaken me. I open my eyes and turn to Sky. My Queen is resting silently. I get up slowly, making sure that I do not disturb true beauty at rest. I walk into the shower. Steam swallows my naked flesh. The hot water cleanses my body so that I am properly bathed of all impurities.

I am lathered in soap from head to toe. I thoroughly rinse my body for her. Once I get out of the shower, the mirrors are unfogged in a matter of seconds. I don't use a towel to dry my body. I naturally air-dry. I begin shaving my face. She likes a smooth surface when she places her hands or face across mine.

As I walk across the bedroom, she is still silently asleep. I step into the walk-in closet, where the doors automatically close behind me. I grab a suit and take it deeper into the closet until I reach an enclosed area surrounded by mirrors.

I begin to clothe my bare flesh. Every piece of clothing must fit to perfection. After all, this day belongs to her. I tie my shoes and make sure the cufflinks are perfect. I look at my watch; it is nearing 3:00 a.m. Right on time. I take one final look in the mirror. While I can see many flaws, my goal is for her to see none.

When I walk into the kitchen, the lights are automatically turned on but kept dim. I pick up a small white linen towel and place it over my shoulder. I cut an apple into three slices, sprinkling the bottom slice with nutmeg, bits of cranberries, and sesame seeds. I place the middle slice on top of it and add a few almonds with a touch of honey. I set the last piece of apple on top and put the apple sandwich on a plate.

I look at the time. I ask Gesture to begin running the bath at 102°
with lavender and juniper as scents. Moments later, Gesture starts
the bath with lavender and juniper dripped all around.

I cut more fruit for Sky, placing strawberries, kiwis, blueberries,
and sliced bananas on a plate with a bowl of cream. The time is
nearing. When I return upstairs, I find my universe peacefully
asleep. I place a small vase of baby's breath on the table next to her.
It is fitting that the flowers' meaning is innocence and purity of
heart.

I slowly kneel down to my sleeping beauty and begin to touch
her face softly. She moves her head slightly before finally opening
her eyes. She smiles.

"Ian? Why are you all dressed up?"

I place my hands over her lips. I so badly want to kiss her, but
it's not time.

"Don't speak. Just come with me."

As Sky gets up, I take her hand and lead her to the bathroom.
The doors automatically open as the scent of lavender and juniper
fill the room. Steam rises from the water. I let go of her hand, take
off my jacket, and roll up my sleeves. I place my hand in the water.
The temperature is perfect.

I walk over to her and begin to undress her. While there are only
two pieces of clothing to remove, I find myself fighting my carnal
instinct to take her into my arms. Nevertheless, I fight back my
emotions and escort her to the tub, where I hold her hand as I guide
her into the steamy water.

As she lies in the scented tub, I pour water across her back and
neck. Then I slowly push her head back to pour water down her hair.

She closes her eyes as the warm water soothes her. I begin to bathe this perfect woman with a sponge, washing around and between all areas of her body. She is so soft everywhere. I can feel her eyes looking at me as I bathe every part of her.

From behind her, I begin to wash her hair, gently massaging her scalp. I can see her shoulders relax as she lets a small moan escape from her mouth. I rinse her hair with the warm water and help her to stand in the tub.

When she steps out, steam rises from her body. I dab the water droplets from her skin with a towel. As I begin to dress her with a white t-shirt, she stops me, reaches for my tie, and begins to loosen it. I shake my head no. She smiles as she reaches for a button on my shirt and taps on it.

I smile.

I take off my tie and put my tailored shirt on her. She leans into the collar to breathe me in. I lather my hands with lotion and coat her entire skin with it. No part of her may be missed—not on *this* day.

I am on my knees as I apply lotion to her inner thighs. I slowly rise, open her shirt, and apply the lotion to all of her chest. The touch brings out a carnal side of her. Her eyes are filled with love, passion, and fire. She wants to devour me with her eyes, but she fights back her basic need to satisfy her appetite.

I sit her down, gently brushing her hair stroke by stroke. As I gently pull back her hair, I whisper in her ear, "Almost time, my love."

She looks at my reflection in the mirror, growing impatient as she is ready to be fed.

I lead her down the stairs to the kitchen, where the lights remain dim. I lift her onto the counter. Looking at my watch, I dip a strawberry into the cream. As I raise it toward her mouth, she opens it.

"Wait," I whisper to her.

She licks her lips in anticipation.

My watch emits a soft chime. It is exactly 4:33 a.m.

I look at her, and with my left hand, I touch the side of her face.

"Happy Birthday, my love," I whisper.

I lean in to taste this forbidden fruit that I have been fighting to have for myself. But I fight no more. She wraps her legs around me and pulls me in.

"Feed me!" she cries.

When I place the strawberry in her mouth, I can hear the crispy crunch as she bites down.

She licks her lips. "Best… birthday… ever."

My forbidden fruit is pleased.

# Our First

I sit at the edge of the pier, petting Mena. I can see my breath on this cold night. I watch the ripples of water float across the lake. Today is a day I want to forget. This was going to happen, as it does in all relationships. All couples must go through this. Be it because of money, family, sex, work, kids, or infidelity, the list can go on till the end of time—and time has chosen for us to have our first fight. My only concern is that we are apart, and I don't like the feeling.

She is inside an empty house that is meant to be filled by two people, and right now, I am on the outside, looking in.

It's not pride that is keeping me from entering the house. I'm giving her space and respecting her wish to walk away from me. But that space between us is a void that I want to fill as quickly as possible. Whatever lengths I have to go to fill that emptiness, I will. However long it takes, I will put in the time.

The silence between us is a disease whose only cure is for us to come together. When we are one, there is nothing that can stop us. Apart, we are weak and fall easily. I cannot allow that. I have to go to her. I must.

When I walk into the house, I feel like a stranger in my own home. In some respects, I am. I could ask Gesture where she is, but I know exactly where she is.

Silence fills every room that I pass as I make my way to the stairs.

With every step I take, I feel the weight of our fight, but I carry the cross as my penance.

As I walk into the bedroom, the very scene of our first fight, everything is in place and in order, but the people in the room are in chaos.

She is standing outside on the balcony. The cold wind blows inside the bedroom.

I walk over, pull the drapes to one side, and stand behind her. She shivers in silence.

I place my hands on the side of her arms and pull her into me, embracing her with my warmth. But that is not all I am embracing her with. I am telling her with my body that I am sorry, that I love her, and that I want this to end now.

She turns around to show me her world of blue. I look into her eyes and stare into that world. She is beaten down, troubled, and worried. She tries to say something, but I stop her. It is I who must say it.

In the natural order of things, it is the Queen who bows before her King, but I toss aside that notion. It is I who bows before my Queen. She is the reason I exist. She is the reason I have my kingdom. She is the reason for my *everything*.

I touch the side of her face softly. In the act of love and war, I gladly allow my walls to crumble and surrender to her.

I hold on to her tighter.

"I'm sorry," I whisper.

She looks into my eyes with grace.

"No, *I* must surrender."

I feel the tightness of her arms as she embraces me.

We surrender to each other.

We surrender for love.

We surrender so the healing can begin.

# She Awakens

The white sand is supposed to be bright here, but it is not. In the distance, I see her walking on water. Do my eyes fool me again, or is she truly a goddess? Above me, the clouds pull rank and cover the skies, no longer allowing the sun to come to us.

The birds are fewer than before. The once-calm winds are beginning to stir the ocean. I feel a tap on my shoulder.

"Sir," said an employee of the hotel, "you and the Mrs. should really take shelter."

I look over to the horizon. She is standing there unafraid, toe to toe, against a force much bigger than herself. She does not flinch. Instead, she smiles.

"Thank you," I say to the employee, "we'll be fine."

I leave the white sandy beach of the Maldives and walk out to join her. I swim for a few yards. The water is choppy, and the surges are growing bigger. My feet touch the bottom, so I can walk to her now.

The winds increase, water splashes over and around me. The storm will do what it can to prevent me from getting to her. I commend its efforts, but it is a losing battle. I am slowly walking up an embankment.

She is now within my reach. The winds gust violently in anger, the thunder echoes its displeasure, and the lightning storm shows its rage.

I, too, am walking on water. I come to my universe and embrace her tightly. We stand in the middle of a storm that would be sure to wipe us from the face of this Earth, but we stand as one with no fear.

She lets go of me and walks away toward the storm. The winds pick up speed, and the surges now grow stronger, and yet we both remain calm in the eye of the storm. I follow her with focus.

She turns to me and places her hand on her black necklace, touching the gray pearl that sits in the middle of it.

An oval pod comes from the ground with powerful blowers to wash away the water. My universe and I enter the pod as we immediately descend into the earth.

We arrive in a room below the Indian Ocean. She walks in front of me. Above us is a clear dome. Stingrays and fish encircle us. I see the storm right above us, yet the noise and power are all gone.

I look to my one and only. She takes off all her clothes, placing the necklace to the side. Her back is to me. The outline of her silhouette is mesmerizing. She turns to me and opens her eyes. Her world of blue lights up my soul.

I come to my goddess and take her into my arms, reaching around to slightly pull her hair. She closes her eyes to show her pleasure.

The ocean bashes against the glass dome but cannot get in.

I make love to my goddess. I make love to her in a storm that only awakens the fire within. She craves my body, my lips, and my soul. We are wrapped together like an inseparable element of life.

# Limelight

It is Fashion Week in the Hamptons. Anybody who is somebody will be there since it is one of the biggest red carpet-events for fashion designers all over the world. In all the years I've been invited, I've never taken the time to accept the invitation. However, this year will be different.

Numerous models will walk the runway, but there is only one face I will be most interested to see, my wife's. She has been asked by several fashion designers to model their latest lines. Versace, Stella McCartney, Tom Ford, Elle, and many more.

I have never been one to seek the spotlight. It has always been my nature to be as far as possible away from the limelight. But this time, the light will be shown on Sky, and I am only too happy to see her shine.

I sit in the front of the runway, a most coveted spot among celebrities, buyers, fashion designers, and people from the music industry. I myself have no vested interest in any designer's line. I just want to see my Queen make her debut as a model.

The lights are dimmed, the music begins to play, and it is Showtime! After a brief introduction by the designer, the models make their way onto the runway. Their strides are long, one foot in front of the other as if they are walking a tightrope. This technique allows them to move their hips from side to side, producing that classic model walk.

Camera flashes come from every direction. Sometimes the lights are so bright that they are blinding. Nevertheless, I am focused. As I said, my eyes belong to her.

At last, I see the one woman who commands all my attention. She is wearing a red dress that is cut like a *V* and flows all around her. The silver pumps she is wearing illuminate her walk. The flashes come in abundance, and just like that, she is gone.

She comes out several more times, and each time she is more gorgeous than before. I am finding it hard to contain my emotions for her. I so badly want this woman in my arms with our lips pressed together.

As I sit there, I begin to concentrate, making the audience go silent, blacked out from the foreground. I slowly erase the other models from the runway, focusing only on her.

We are alone together. She models for me, smiles for me and spins around for me. My love grows impatient as I see her time after time, but only for a few seconds. It is a tease to the senses, which I do not like.

I see her coming toward me again. This time she will not walk away. I get up out of my chair and walk to the edge of the runway. She is the definition of true beauty. The bar cannot be set any higher than her. If it could, it would have to be God.

She stands in front of me, looking down at me. As I step onto the runway, she begins to laugh.

"What are you doing?" she asks.

I gently touch the side of her face.

"You are the most beautiful woman I have ever laid eyes on."

I lean in to kiss her. Her lips are soft, wet, and plentiful.

When I return to reality, the flashes are as bright as the sun. Maybe the limelight isn't all that bad, so long as she is by my side.

# My Savior

We are coming home from a charity event. She asks Gesture to exit the highway and go to a certain business.

"Why do you want to go there?" I ask, looking at her.

"You remember when we first saw each other?"

"Yes."

"That night, I was making plans to go away for a long time and never come back."

"Plans to go where?"

She just stares at me and remains silent.

I touch the side of her face.

"No, my love," I say. "Why would you even think about something so horrible?"

"I did, but, for whatever reason, fate made me look to my right, and there you were as you passed my table. You, a stranger, had an expression on your face that told me you were looking for something. The look you gave me broke me, dissected me, and sent warmth through my body. You brought me back from the brink, Ian."

"And you brought me back from mine."

"You will never know how much I love you, how much I truly love you. I would give you anything you want."

"I only want you."

As we arrive at the business, she smiles.

"I'm going in alone," she says. "Wait five minutes. Then come in after me."

"Why do I have to wait five minutes? Let's just go in together."

"Just give me five minutes. That's all I ask."

"Why?"

"Please," she whispers

I look into her sea of blue calmness.

"Okay…. Five minutes."

She opens the door, turns to me, and smiles. As she shuts the door behind her, I watch her go into this establishment that brings back so many memories of *that* night. Five minutes of her being alone in there is something I can barely stomach. I only came here that one time because I was trying to kill time. Now we are here because she wants to be here.

Five minutes pass, but it feels like years, and I have aged without my fountain of youth next to me. I get out of the car. Gesture parks the car as the doors to the strip club are opened for me. The same bass I felt over a year ago penetrates me and my clothes. The vibration shakes my senses.

I search her out, but I cannot find her. A young woman grabs my arm. Then another young woman grabs my other arm.

"She is waiting for you," they both say.

They walk me through the crowd of hollering men.

They lead me through a door. When it closes, the sound from the other part of the club vanishes. The room is solid red with dimmed lights. At one end, there is a chair that is made for a King. Its back is high, and its armrests are carved into two lions painted gold.

The young women escort me to the chair.

"Enjoy," they say as they touch the side of my face.

Then they both leave the room.

I can only hear my own breath.

The lights dim even more. Music begins to play. I search for what comes next, but all I can see is darkness.

When the bass starts to hit, erotic lyrics run all over my body.

The line "Don't stop looking at me" is a haunting hook that is embedded in my mind.

I look around the room. Then, across from me, I see something that reminds me of home. Her eyes glow brighter than ever. All I can see is her blue oasis. She steps forward from the darkness.

Her soft white creamy skin is flaming, and her hair is fiery red. Her entire body is painted black and red. She walks slowly toward me as a pole descends from above. She places her hand on the pole and walks around it twice before finally jumping on it.

The strength of her arms and legs is immediately visible. This woman is not human. With a body like hers, she is a goddamn goddess. She moves like the water of oceans. Her hair drips and flows like the wind. Her eyes are a blue fire that stirs my soul in a glass. I cannot stop looking at her.

As she walks quickly toward me, her breasts bounce with each hard step. When she stops in front of me, I gaze at her body, which is yearning for me. I can hear all my emotions screaming out for her. I am being ravaged inside as the beast from within is ready to take over and eat this woman whole.

She bends over and places her finger on my chest. The beast from within roars, begging to be released from its hell into this paradise called Sky.

She opens her legs, slowly gets on top of me, and straddles my body.

She looks at me intently as she runs her hands down her neck and across her breasts, pushing them together. Her cup runneth over.

I place my hand over her neck, and she places hers over mine. I pull her down to me.

"There is nothing I wouldn't give you," my goddess says.

I look at this woman who once contemplated suicide. I don't know what I would do without her now. She is my life, my world, my universe. I would go to whatever ends it takes to make her happy, to make her smile, to make her feel loved.

I loosen my grip around her neck and run my hand down her breasts.

She stops my hand where her heart is, firmly pressing her hand against mine,

"Never let go," she whispers in my ear.

"I promise, my love… Never."

She is my savior more than I am hers. Our paths have crossed at the right time in our lives—a time when love can be rediscovered, when love illuminates us inside and saves us both from the abyss.

# Exploration

I have made love to exactly two women in my lifetime, and how I wish it were only with one. The moon is bright this late at night. Sky lies naked on top of me. Her bare skin is warm and smooth. I touch her hair. I can feel her breathing softly. Her heart beats in synch with mine.

I look at her legs. The surface is beyond any man's imagination. The curves she possesses are too great to be controlled, but each and every time, I find a way to do so. I run my fingers down the sides of her legs. I have never felt something so unbearably smooth and refined.

My fingers lead to another curve, a curve that takes a sharp ninety degrees down to where she still remains wet. I come up slowly to the side of her thighs. There she is, thick. There is where I love to dig into her, but I do not. Instead, I allow my Queen to rest.

I now place my hand where the land is plentiful and absolutely gorgeous. It is firm, tight, and, for lack of a better word, juicy. I squeeze gently, but just enough to fill the tips of my fingers. I let go of this beautiful and plentiful surface and continue my journey up her back.

I feel the sensual dimples of Venus on her backside.

The plains of her back are smooth from every angle, but beneath the smooth terrain, she is strong. She is built to withstand, she is built to carry whatever rests on her shoulders, she is built like no other.

I leave this place of strength for another place that is equally strong. Her arms are slender, but again, to mistake these arms for anything less would be ignorant. As I run my hand down her arm, I feel that she is cold.

I grab the comforter and pull it on top of us. I rest my head and stare at the moonlight shining through the skylight. I feel her body getting warmer. The rays from the moon suddenly turn blue. I look down at her. She is awake. She looks at me with love and disappointment.

"What is it, my love?" I ask.

"Are you done?"

"Am I done doing what?"

She throws off the comforter.

"Never," I say, smiling.

She reaches for me and kisses me. My journey through her body and soul begins yet again.

# Yes

We are on the outskirts of San Antonio. Through donations, she purchased two thousand acres of land for one reason—*hope.*

The land is bountiful and full of energy. Dogs and cats are roaming and running free, experiencing the pure pleasure of being outdoors. People come from all over the state to adopt a pet.

Sky plays with their kids as they chase the small puppies, who give Sky and the kids many wet kisses. I can see her happiness, I can see her laughing, I can see what a beautiful soul she has.

Sky made all this possible through charity events she organized. She wanted to showcase every animal that was there and worked tirelessly to get every single dog and cat a new home.

Her efforts did not go in vain.

Every Sunday, the turnout was greater than the previous one. Hundreds of volunteers worked the site as they helped with adopting, cleaning, feeding, and caring for the animals. There are pools, play skills areas, picnic areas, and even hydrotherapy areas for rehabilitating animals that are learning to walk again.

I watch from a distance under a shady tree. Mena sits next to me and watches people as they play with the puppies. I am happy to see animals and human beings with one another, but I look at one human in particular, watching her as she plays with the children and the puppies. I watch as her laughter is tireless, and her energy is overflowing.

I wonder if I am holding her back from having something of her own, something that I have never wanted—a child. I reach down to pet Mena, who looks up at me. She is sitting calmly next to me, but inside, she is a bundle of joy and energy that is waiting for me to set free.

"Do you want to go play, Mena?"

Her tail begins to wag. I bend down.

"Have fun, my girl."

Before I can say one more word, she sprints toward Sky. Mena is careful around the pups but pushes some out of the way to get to Sky.

I laugh as they play together.

The kids grab for Mena, who is just a big ball of fur, and she lets them play with her. She is gentle with the kids and even gives a few of them kisses, but she is there to be around a woman who is a mother to her in her eyes.

The word *mother* is strong in every language, as it should be. I wonder once again if that is what Sky wants in the future. She is still young and may want a child, but the subject has never come up, which may be because of my past. I have never wanted children for fear that they will be like my father, who killed my mother on my birthday. His blood still runs through mine. No matter how much I don't want it to be there, it is.

I love Sky with everything I have. There is nothing I wouldn't do to make her happy. As I watch the joy on her face while she plays with the children, I ask myself, *Will I ever give her a child if she asks? Will I ever give her the joy of holding her own?*

I think about the man I have become and what I have accomplished. I have done more in this lifetime than I could have ever hoped for, and I have been paired with the greatest woman any man could ever want.

When I return to the now, I look at this woman who brought me in from the darkness and breathed life into me. It was the greatest feeling I have ever felt, and for me to experience that alone would be selfish. She would be the greatest mother, with a heart so filled with love and joy that the child would grow up to be a monument to her.

I feel joy inside myself. I feel like a kid again. Sky is my fountain of youth, and that youth wants to play.

I run from the shadows onto the ground where she is. I run to her, to my one true love, to my wife.

I come from behind her. When she turns around, she is winded. She smiles at me. I reach for her and kiss her. I can feel the puppies jumping all over us, but I continue to kiss this woman who has captured more than my heart and soul.

Yes. The answer is yes.

# One Love

I love coming to this tiny Greek island called Fournoi. It's been a long time, but it has remained as beautiful as ever. The sand is soft, the breeze coming off the water is cool, and the night is calm. Our only companion is the moon.

A dark silhouette emerges from the water. When she pushes back her hair, the water flows down her natural curves. As she opens her eyes, her blue havens stir my soul yet again.

The moon stands watch behind her. When she turns to face the cratered white giant, she stands tall, like a force of nature to be reckoned with. The love of my life compliments the water, moon, and stars.

When she fell from the heavens, of all the people she could have crashed into, she crashed into me. And when she did, she didn't allow me to leave her thoughts. And that is why we share a single heartbeat together.

She turns her head to look over her shoulder as if to see if she is alone or in company. We were both alone at one time, but now we are the only ones with a key to the other's heart.

The dark silhouette calls my name. I rise from the crust of the Earth and walk over to the center of the universe. I walk toward where life begins—and ends.

She is a being of light. At first, she is dim, but as I get closer, her strength grows, as does mine. The moon becomes bigger, and the water begins to churn and rise as I approach the center of the universe—the center of *my* universe.

I feel the power of our love shaking the Earth's core. This type of love is immeasurable in power and in strength. This type of love is only experienced in the next lifetime, but maybe we are *already* in the next lifetime, and we are just realizing all our strengths as one.

I come from behind this beautiful and elegant universe. I come to her with no fear, with no hesitation, but with body, mind, and soul open to engulf this being of light.

As I embrace her, a light so bright comes from both of us. The light is so immense and powerful that it breathes life into the universe. Our love stretches out to every corner of darkness, conquers all fears, and gives humanity hope that love can and will overcome any obstacle.

In front of the white giant, I hold on to my universe, my wife, my reason for being.

# The Thought

I am in a boardroom meeting. Something is on my mind as I turn my wedding ring around my finger. I stare out the window, looking at the city. Something is not right. I can feel the beginnings of worry take over my thoughts.

I don't know what it is, but it troubles me.

I reach for my phone. There are no missed texts or phone calls. My mind and heart begin to think of *her*.

I look at the time. It's been over four hours since I've seen her smile, felt her kiss, or held her close to me. It's been four hours too long.

The conference is filled with chatter, but I am lost and confused about the feelings I'm having. I am nervous, anxious, scared, and upset. I look at the blue bottle of Ty Nant Water set to the side of me. I can only think of her blue eyes.

The boardroom meeting is interrupted by a phone call.

Nia picks up the phone and looks over at me.

"It's for you, Ian."

I go to the corner of the boardroom, which is more private. I pick up the phone, but the only words I hear are *wife, accident, hurt, sustained,* and *transport.*

As I drop the phone and start to leave, I hear questions being asked and my name being called, but the one voice I want to hear is not here.

As Gesture drives me to the hospital, I'm an emotional mess. I cannot keep up with my feelings and emotions. I cannot think straight. I am silent, and yet my silence is the loudest sound.

Rain starts to pour from above. I touch the window. During the hardest times in my life, it has always rained. I begin to see images of her on the window. I reach out to her. I tell her that I am almost there. I tell her I love her.

I cannot endure the thought of losing my universe. The love I have is too great for me to be left alone without her. She is everything. My only reason for being here during this lifetime is to make her happy. I cannot fail this one task that has been given to me.

I am already out the door before the car even comes to a complete stop. I walk into the emergency room, bypassing everyone and going straight to the triage area.

A young nurse tells me I need to wait.

She tells me to calm down.

She tells me to lower my voice.

I have never been so insane in all my life. I feel hands grab my arms and come across my chest.

*Do they dare keep me from my universe?*

I rip away the hands that try to bind me and break the hold from my chest. There is no force so great that it can keep me from her, and if there is, it will have to take my last breath away, for I will not go down without a fight.

The nurse comes over and begs me to stop.

I momentarily black out.

She raises her voice, but I can't hear what she is saying, nor can I see her.

When I regain full consciousness, I try to calm down.

Again and again, she asks me to stop.

Finally, my vision returns, and I can see her.

"Sky," I whisper.

The nurse says something and leaves. Around me are bodies that slowly get up from the floor. I try to brush this apprehension from my thoughts. I try to gather the composure that I, Ian Branch, am known for.

The nurse returns.

"Follow me," she says.

I follow her. I pass room after room, looking into each carefully so that I don't pass my true love.

The nurse stops at a room and points inside.

I slowly come around and look in. Sky is lying on her side, asleep.

I slowly walk in so as not to disturb my universe. She is resting so peacefully that, for a brief moment, I am scared. I kneel down next to her. I look at her armband.

"Sky Branch" is typed in bold black letters.

I run my fingers across the armband. I run my fingers across the tips of her fingers. The moment I do, I can feel her heartbeat. I run my fingers ever so softly across her lips and on the side of her face.

I stare at my universe.

I count the number of her breaths.

I count the number of her eyelashes.

I count the number of seconds for her to show me her world of blue.

My touch finally awakens her.

She opens her eyes.

"I am here, my love."

# Now and in the Next

I am sitting at my desk, going through reports, research and development revenue, dividend yields, and gross domestic product analysis while watching live coverage of the presidential election. One of my best friends, who also went to Yale, is running for his second term in office.

As I look at the latest numbers, he is pulling ahead in electoral votes. Another thirty-three electoral votes and my old pal from college will be serving his second term, and I will be serving another four years as a member of his cabinet—his "Kitchen Cabinet," that is.

I am jotting down some things on a piece of paper when I see a glass of red wine set down before me. She is so stealthy that I didn't hear her enter my study. She is wearing a black nightgown that I can see right through.

She sits down in a leather chair across from me. She crosses her legs and takes a sip of her wine.

"You think men could run the world without women by their side?" she asks.

I put down my pen.

"No, not even for one revolution."

"Why is that?"

"The center of existence is a woman's heart. Her heart is what defines our world. Without you to guide us, we men would be lost in darkness."

"So, the sole purpose of a man is to serve a woman?"

"Not just serve, but love and protect. Without women, the purpose of living becomes mute. What drives us is the wanting and affection that we men must have."

"Is that what drives you now?"

I get up from behind my desk, walk over to her, grab her hand, and kneel before her.

"What drives me, my love, is far more than a woman. You give me reason, you give me hope, and you give me all that I need to be happy and to make you happy."

She puts her glass aside, looks deep within me, touches my face, and says:

*When you are weary, I will be your rock to sit upon.*

*When you are hurt, I will be your bandage.*

*When you are in darkness, I will be your beacon of light.*

*When you are in doubt, I will be your support.*

*When you are troubled, I will be your comfort.*

*When you fall, I will be there to carry you.*

*When you are scared, I will be your hope.*

*When you are lost, I will be your compass.*

*When you cry, I will be your happiness.*

*But most of all, when you think you are not loved,*

*You are loved like no other.*

This woman, who found a way to my heart and soul, has me in more ways than just one. I devote all of my love to her, right down to my last breath and my last beat.

I reach for her face, touch her softly, and kiss her red lips of life.

"Ian, my love," she says, "we were apart at one time in our lives, but never again. Now, and in the next, I will forever be yours."

I pick up my universe from the chair and take her into my arms. I carry her to the bedroom. The doors close behind us. I lay her on the bed gracefully. I slowly climb on top of her.

I kiss every part of her. Every part is just as important as the next.

I am finally eye to eye with my universe, my true love.

"Now, and in the next… I promise, my love."

I kiss her passionately, I kiss her lovingly, and I kiss her for the rest of my life.

# Home

I am asleep on the couch. I am dreaming, yet I have no idea what I am dreaming about. My body is tired, my mind is restless, and my soul is weary.

Suddenly, I feel myself being pulled from my incoherent dream and back into the realm of now.

A touch is what brings me from my darkness. As I slowly open my eyes, my universe is running her hands through my hair. She is sitting next to me, peering into my soul. I allow myself to be absorbed fully by her.

Her touch is slow and defined, heaven-sent. I look into her eyes, which are as blue as the sea. Her face is so pure, and her smile so soothing to the soul. I reach for the side of her face. The touch of her skin is truly a once-in-a-lifetime experience.

I run my finger across her lips, which are moist and full. The Red Sea would be stripped of its name if compared to her lips.

She says my name. Her voice, with my name on her lips, penetrates every part of my body. I close my eyes, take in a deep breath, and consume every part of her voice and breath within me. I can feel them enter my body. I can feel them caressing my heart, sending chills throughout my soul, and yet sending warmth over me that is truly unbelievable.

My universe continues holding me, touching me, loving me. In all my life, I have never let my guard down, except for her. To her, I will surrender everything. I will show her my faults, my secrets, my pains, my passions, and my love.

She leans in, closes her eyes, and kisses me on the lips. The red sea is soft, barely touching my lips, yet I am blessed with life and emotion beyond measure.

She pulls away, but I cannot let her escape. She is only inches from me, but I must keep this angel of a woman near me.

She is my savior, my breath, my heart, my soul, my friend, and my wife.

As I slowly pull her to me once again, she smiles. Her eyes glow with pure happiness. My whole universe comes to me, takes me in, protects me, breathes life into me, and surrounds me with her love.

She is everything that I want and more. But more than anything, she is where the heart is.

She is my home.

# The Moon

We walk the Isle of Lewis in Scotland. Today is special since she wants to see the supermoon. For this to occur, the sun, moon, and Earth must be aligned. She has always been fascinated with the moon, as if they have an unbreakable bond.

We walk hand in hand. She is completely lost in the white giant above us. I let her go of her hand and watch as she stares at the cratered moon.

Then she looks at me.

With her blue eyes penetrating my soul, she says, "Write me something."

As I look at her, words cannot describe what I feel. Yet, I begin to speak to her heart and soul under the white giant:

*She glows under the moon.*

*She waits under the moon, her guardian.*

*She opens her heart.*

*She lets the blood flow freely.*

*She is exposed under her guardian.*

*She looks to the moon and begins to cry.*

*Tears of happiness and frustration flow down her face.*

*She waits....*

*She waits….*

*She waits for him under the moon.*

*She grows tired, weak, and near breathless.*

*She begins to break.*

*She begins to falter.*

*She fades under the watch of her guardian.*

*She turns to the moon, her guardian.*

*She smiles one last time and begins her descent.*

*She never touches the ground.*

*She is being caressed.*

*She is being protected.*

*She no longer fights this battle alone.*

*He looks down at her, "Never will you fall."*

*He kisses her under the moon.*

*He touches her under the moon.*

*He came to her, guided only by the moon.*

# Cold and Hot

After my final lap, I lie against the edge of the infinity pool, staring at a house I bought in Norway many years ago but have never visited. Huge glass windows encompass the house. Privacy is something that is not acknowledged by this house. Maybe that is why I could never see myself visiting or staying there.

I see her walking around in her long white t-shirt with Mena closely behind her. I smile as the closest thing Sky has to a child is Mena, and the closest thing to a mother that Mena has is Sky. They completely love and adore each other.

Behind the house of glass lie the mountains of Norway, covered in snow. Above me are the same stars wherever I go, and close enough to me is her guardian in full view. He has been through a lot, as I have. I know his stories as he knows mine, every single one of them.

Steam comes off the water as it hits the cold air. I lay my head back to stare at the stars. The lights from the house begin to turn off, room by room. I search for her and Mena, but the lights continue to turn off.

The entire house is now in darkness. I ask Gesture to turn on the lights of the house. Gesture does not comply.

Suddenly, the large bay windows in the back of the house begin to retract. Above the windows, white luminescent water flows where the windows once stood. A silhouette begins to appear behind a waterfall.

The silhouette is unlike any other. She stands there in silence. When she opens her eyes, the water begins to turn light blue. She raises her arms above her and takes off her shirt.

She waits….

She reaches with one hand through the waterfall, feeling the water as if it were alien to her. She slowly steps forward under the waterfall. The water runs down her natural naked curves. She pulls her hair back to one side.

The goddess draws the attention of the universe from the stars above, which begin to shine brighter.

My body temperature begins to rise, as does the steam from the water. I lose sight of my universe. I begin to make my way through the water.

She now stands naked in front of the pool.

She stares at me.

I stare back.

There is nothing that she wants to hide from me, nothing that she won't expose to me. I see all of her. I see more than her body. I see her blood flowing, her thoughts revealing. But more importantly, I see her heart beating.

It beats in synch with mine.

She smiles and begins to walk into the pool. As she makes her way down the steps, the lights around the pool turn to a dark blue.

I stand frozen as this beautiful angel makes her way to me.

She stands in front of me, with water trickling down her face. Her eyes please me in more ways than one. Her lips are full of color, like that of a cherry red apple. I step closer to my temptation.

She invites me in with a smile. I gladly accept her invitation. I grab her and pull her body up against mine.

She willingly gives in to me.

I look up at her guardian, who is suddenly bigger and closer.

I nod my head, acknowledging that she is well taken care of.

I touch the side of her face.

She closes her eyes.

I kiss her under the heavens.

I kiss her under her guardian.

# Harley Quinn

A world of black attire surrounds me this night. Heroes, demons, and paint all hide the faces but not the person. I can hear the ticks of a clock continuing its natural, consistent right turn. Laughter, voices, and screams surround me.

I, too, hide behind a mask. My suit is dark, my shirt white, my vest black, and my cloak as dark as night. It hangs inches from the floor. But the mask that hides me is that of a phantom. *The Phantom of the Opera.*

My identity is hidden, but that does not stop the women of the night as they clamor and claw to have a picture taken with the Phantom on this hallowed night.

The flashes and the smiles are enduring, but I continue my search for my one and only.

My universe.

I walk through the massive house in search of her. The moon leads me outside. I walk to the edge of the property. I see wave after wave crashing onto the rocks. When I look above, I see my old friend and her guardian. I acknowledge him and assure him I will find her.

I look out onto the waters. I listen to the sound of the ocean. I close my eyes and take in a deep breath. I am alive. Something in me feels as if I have been given a purpose. I can smell her scent. I can hear her heartbeat.

When I turn around, my universe is standing on the other side of the infinity pool, holding a bat over her shoulder. Her hair is white and green with two ponytails. The tips of one are red, the other blue. She is chewing gum with confidence.

Her flawless, defined thighs appear through transparent black lace. Tattoos cover her legs that my hands and lips have touched countless times. Her shirt hugs her frame and shows how busty she is. Her shirt reads, "Daddy's Lil Monster," which I now have a fondness for.

Her face is painted, but it is the smeared red lipstick that screams at me. She has a revolver next to her left arm. The revolver has white inlaid grips. Her shorts do not leave much to the imagination as they ride high and hug her hips.

She draws a crowd. Men want to eat her alive, and women envy her. Nevertheless, I go to my vixen.

She follows me with her eyes. Her confidence grows with her smile. I am no Joker per se, but I am *her* Joker.

I stand in front of her. She chews her gum while smiling.

"What?" she asks

"You know you're fucking amazing, right?"

She pivots back and forth with the bat still behind her head.

"I know, Daddy."

I lean down and kiss my vixen.

I lean down and kiss the total opposite of me.

I lean down and kiss my Harley Quinn.

# Thunder and Rain

The car door is open. Sky gets in, followed by me. The door closes automatically behind us. I give Gesture the command to go home. The car is autopiloted back home. We are leaving an award ceremony in which Sky was recognized as San Antonio's Woman of the Year.

It is late. Her guardian is out in full view, but a rainstorm is approaching. I can hear the thunder rattling the city. I am proud of my universe and her achievements. She looks ravishing this late at night.

I don't think I have told her enough.

She is sitting on a dark gray leather captain's chair. I am sitting opposite her. The lighting inside the vehicle is low. Black wool carpet lines the floor beneath our feet. She stares at me. I stare back at her. She smiles. I smile back.

My universe begins to let her hair down, and as she does, rain begins to fall. She takes out clip after clip from her hair, each one inviting the rain to drop harder.

As we begin to leave the city lights behind, she runs her finger across the center panel. When she does, the lights are turned off, and the dark tint in the windows is gone. I look above me and see lightning illuminating the sky in every direction. Winds are blowing clouds around like feathers. Raindrops are now crashing upon us. In the distance, he is there, always watching.

I turn to her, to my universe. I watch as the shadows of the rain run across her entire body. Lightning strikes across the night sky, highlighting her blue magnificence. She begins to pull her dress off her shoulder.

She pauses, runs her finger across her lips, smiles, and then continues to disrobe for me.

She lies down on the black wool. She moves like a serpent, elevating my senses to a level that is beyond comprehension. She opens her legs to me. I see her pink valley. She is wet, like the Amazon, and I have yet to touch her.

We are naked to all the elements around us. I slowly place my body on top of hers. I breathe her in. The oils from our bodies bind to one another. We are inseparable. I look deep into her world, gently touching the side of her face. I kiss her softly. I place my hand across her neck. She breathes in a small sigh and smiles.

I enter my universe. She opens her mouth. She is breathless. Thunder and lightning perform a symphony so beautiful that her guardian takes solace behind the clouds. I make love to my wife as only she deserves.

I make love to her thoughts, her heart, and her soul.

I touch her so that she feels all of me so that she can experience my love, a love so powerful that it encompasses all of her, protects her, and worships her.

I am one with my wife.

I am one with my universe.

# A Desert Night

I am awakened with a soft whisper. I open my eyes. The tent breathes in the coolness from the outside. The white and black sashes blow from side to side. I turn to Sky, and she is once again gone. Mena is fast asleep in her bed of cushioned pillows.

I arise from bed. The crackling of the fire is low. It is starving and needs to be fed. Her robe is the only thing missing. I grab my robe and walk outside. Nothing is there.

I look at the sand as it tells a story through its twists and turns in the wind. While I would like to know its story, my only concern is my universe. The night is bright this evening, more so than usual. I look over the horizon, and he is there, but something is different.

He is calm as he glows blue. I don't know where she is, and yet I'm not worried. My sight fails to see where she is, and yet I know where she is. I *always* know where she is.

Above me is a giant sand dune.

She is up there, and while the desert may wash away all memory of her, it cannot wash away the love that drives me. I begin to ascend the giant dune. My feet sink into the sand. My impression is left but then erased within seconds.

The desert sand is unforgiving, demanding everything from me, including my memories. I can feel the bite of the cool air as it races across my body. The desert kicks sand in my face as a passive-aggressive reminder that it can take me any time it wants.

And it probably could, but not on this night. The sand beneath me begins to give, playing with me as I slide down its slopes. I dig into it, although it laughs as it engulfs my arms and feet.

It takes me for a ride, toying with me, but I climb it anyway, refusing to give up. I show it that I am not willing to give up, and just like that, it stops. Maybe it found another soul to take, or maybe it respects what I am trying to do.

The climb is still tough, but it aids me by not letting me slide any longer. When I make it to the top before me is one of the greatest images I have ever seen.

I see Sky. Her hair is flowing as the wind plays with it, almost wanting to tell a story as it does. Her robe flows across her body, but it is what she is doing with her hand that is truly amazing.

She is touching the outer edges of the moon as if it were within reach. The moon glows brighter as if it feels her touch. I can hear whispered words as she talks to him. The words are calm, truthful, and loving, as in a conversation between father and daughter.

I finally understand. I finally know why.

It is not for me to interrupt this moment.

I slowly step away.

Respecting my decision, the giant sand dune forms stairs for me to descend. But after each of my steps, it twists and turns, erasing my footprints.

I walk back into the tent, take off my robe, and walk over to Mena, who is still resting peacefully. I pet her fur. She does not awaken from her deep slumber. I return to bed. I lie there, thinking about Sky. I lie there, thinking about the deep love I have for her. I lie there, thinking….

I am asleep when I smell her scent. She lays her body across mine, slowly touching my chest. I don't know if I am dreaming, but I don't want to open my eyes if I am. I breathe her in. I love the way her hair smells. Her body scent is heavenly.

My body tastes her and hungers for more of her. I feel her head move. She is quiet. I can barely hear her breath. I feel the soft touch of her lips against mine. She is slow, tender, and adoring. I don't yet open my eyes. I don't want this dream to end.

"I love you, Ian."

My universe speaks to me in my dreams.

"I love you, too, Sky."

My universe curls up and wraps her entire body around mine.

Our hearts beat slower, our breaths become shallower. We wrap ourselves around each other. We wrap ourselves in our love. We wrap ourselves because this is what is meant to be.

# A Dance

We are being driven by Gesture to a political fundraiser. I am absolutely in awe of her. She is wearing an elegant gray open-back dress. It is formfitting, showing the beauty of her shoulders. While she is the definition of timeless beauty, there is something wrong with my universe.

She is sitting in silence, staring out the window. I lean over to touch her face. She reacts to my touch with a smile.

"What's wrong, my love?" I ask.

"Nothing."

Something is, and it troubles me. I know my wife. I can see it on her face, but that is not the dead giveaway. I can feel it from within. I know what she is thinking, and I know how I can make her happy.

I lean back to type in a different address on the control panel— a place she had wanted to visit one night while we were downtown. I say nothing of the change as I take her hand, sitting back to let her know that I am here for her.

As we make our way, she squeezes my hand. She looks over at me. My universe smiles at me, and I at her. We park, and I help her out of the car. We walk up to an outside patio that has one food truck and another for wine and spirits.

We approach the teenage hostess. I can immediately tell that no one is there.

"Hi," I say. "What time do you close?"

The hostess looks at her watch.

"Not for another hour. You can sit anywhere you like."

"Thank you."

Sky holds my hand and guides me. Above us are lights intertwined with the vines of the trees, forming a roof. In the middle of the small but quaint establishment, there was an opening above. Sky decides to sit there to be under the stars.

The young hostess comes over.

"You two look so cute together. Almost like you're coming from a homecoming prom."

I look at her name tag.

"Thank you, Elsa."

"Can I get you two some wine?"

"Sure, anything that's red."

"Of course. I know just the one."

"Thank you, Elsa."

My universe looks at me.

"Thank you."

"For what?"

"I know you wanted to go to that event tonight, but I just didn't feel like it. I know that seems selfish, but I just didn't."

"I don't want to be anywhere you don't want to be."

She leans across the table to take my hand.

"It's just that now that I have finally found you," she says, "all I want to do is never leave your side."

"We found each other," I say, "and I will never leave your side."

"You promise?"

"Till the sun dies, my love."

She leans in for a kiss, and I am only too happy to kiss this goddess.

Elsa returns with our red wine.

"Oh, my god! You two are just so adorable!"

My universe blushes, but Elsa is right. Sky is absolutely adorable.

When we raise our glasses, the chime from their touch can be heard across the room. As we take a sip, I notice the glow around her. She is shining so magnificently, but I have seen this glow before. I look above us, and all I can do is smile. I see her looking up as she smiles, too. Her eyes show how much she loves him.

Our moment is interrupted when we hear a loudspeaker come on. Suddenly, music starts to play. Elsa and her companion from the food truck are smiling at us.

I look over at my wife. Saying nothing to her, I walk around the table to her side. When I ask for her hand, she gladly gives it, placing it inside mine. I bring my universe close to my heart.

We dance under the glow of the moon. We dance under the glow of love.

May we dance together, forever.

# The Talk

I am in darkness. I can see, yet I see nothing. I hear my name being called in the distance. The voice is unlike anything I have ever heard or encountered. Silence surrounds me. Again, I hear my name. The voice is calming yet commands great respect.

I am pulled from my sleep by this voice. I open my eyes. I turn to her. She breathes silently. I get up from the bed. I walk over to her and touch the side of her face. I know of the voice that calls me this night, and I know why.

I walk out to the terrace. The night is beautiful, the air is cool, and the heavens sparkle this clear night. He, too, is bright this clear night. I walk out to a single chair located on the terrace. An invitation I was fully expecting.

As I stand, the moon grows in size before my eyes. He knows everything I have ever done in my life, good and bad. He knows when I am being truthful and when I am not. He knows when I am happy and when I am not. He knows everything, and if there is doubt, he will see it.

Before anything can begin, I must first tell of a love that he has seen but not felt or understood. I tell him about a life that was once an empty soul that wandered through life without purpose or reason. A life that was numb to the outside world. A life without emotion.

I was readying myself for complete and total loneliness and wither away, but I would never make it to my destination. I was stopped along the way by a woman who refused to let that happen, a woman who is unlike any other and will never be like her in this lifetime or the next.

I love this woman with all my heart. I would sacrifice my life for that of hers. I would bleed for this woman, and when I say bleed, I would allow my blood to flow from my body like that of the oceans, to the last drop.

I would protect this woman to no end. I would never kneel or surrender to another. I would fight till my last breath, I would fight till the sun dies and the moon turns to rust. I would fight an entire world for just one second with her, for just one look, for just one touch.

I would love this woman till no end. Oceans of this world couldn't quench my love for her, not even, not ever. It would take oceans from unknown worlds beyond that of ours to satisfy my eternal love for her, and even then, that would only be the beginning of what it is to love this woman.

I talk of a love so great that when I kiss her, I kiss life, I kiss love, I kiss a single universe that is only meant for me and I for her. I kiss her a million times before she even wakes up, and when she does, I give her that one kiss that would last a million lifetimes, and that's just to say good morning.

When I hold her, it is a bond so strong and so loving that other worlds would be birthed from our bond. When I hold her, it is so great that time will stop just to pay its respect. When I hold her, monuments would be raised, paintings made, sculptures sculpted, and songs written to honor that of our inseparable bond.

I look up at him as he glows bright. I stand away from my chair and walk closer to him. I close my eyes and take in a deep breath. I open them. I look at him.

Begin.

# Fix You

Night is with us once again. Our helicopter flies over the Indian Ocean on the way to our destination. She wears blue jeans with black high heels and a long purple shirt that is untucked. Simple? Yes, but that's what I love about her.

She sees that I do not like to live this day or celebrate it. She grabs my hand and squeezes it. She looks into my eyes and sees the pain that this day brings me. She truly wants me to forget, and I know she does everything possible to make it happen.

The night so many years ago still haunts me. On my birthday, he took me to a gun shop and told me to choose the gun I liked the most. The one that caught my eye was a 9mm stainless steel handgun.

I still remember him pointing the gun at her head as she slept. Seeing two shots being fired into her and the slow turnaround, and seeing his blood-splattered face. Him slowly kneeling down to face me to tell me that it was my fault that she is dead and that I would never have another mother again.

I've always hated this day.

She leans in and kisses me. She whispers, 'I love you,' and I whisper it right back to her. I smile and look out the window. The night is calm, like that of the ocean. He fades in and out from the clouds. This time, he is distant. This time, he gives me my space.

We circle over a park and land. I help her down from the helicopter. She guides me through the darkness. We come to an open field at the Royal Botanic Gardens in Sydney. There, in the middle of the open field, sits a lone table with a lit candle and two chairs.

I pull the chair out for her, and she takes her seat. I take my chair across from her. The table is small, with barely enough room for our hands to place on. She says nothing but smiles at me. She reaches across and grabs my hand.

Her touch is soft and gentle as she strokes my hand. I enjoy her touch. It is calming and soothing. She does take the pain away from that night, that night so many years ago when I was a child. Only she can take away the pain. It is she that absorbs my pain and takes it as her own.

That's what love is, willing to take away your pain so that you no longer have to carry it or remember it. She reminds me that people like her truly exist, that truly want to give everything to someone and want nothing in return.

I sometimes wonder how and why I was blessed with such a wonderful human being that is now my wife. I sometimes have to pinch myself to make sure this world is real and that she really has chosen me for the rest of her life.

But it is real, her touch lets me know that I am alive, her touch lets me know that this is meant to be. I touch her face as she continues to look at me. God, how I love this woman.

"Ian." She whispers

"Yes, my love."

"Till the moon turns to rust."

"Till the sun dies."

"Do you promise?"

"Always, my love, always."

"Make a wish."

"It already came true."

"I am not your wish, I am your forever."

I smile at the thought of forever with her.

"Make a wish."

I close my eyes and take in a small breath. I wish for only one thing, to make her eternally happy.

I open my eyes. She looks at me.

"Now blow out the candle."

I blow out the candle, and darkness engulfs our moment.

I can barely see her, she leans in and kisses me.

"Happy Birthday," she whispers

I begin to see a small light in the distance. Music begins to play. I hear a voice begin to sing. The song is one of my favorites. The song being sung is 'Fix You' by Coldplay.

I begin to see glow sticks all around the park begin to light up. People come out from the darkness and make their way to us. One of the first faces I see and recognize is Nia, with Mena by her side. I look at the other faces, and they are faces from the company.

Nothing but family surrounds me on this night.

I look at her. I go to her and embrace her tightly. I kiss her with everything I have. Only she could take the pain away, only her love could take away that night.

Tonight, she does that; she replaces it with love and family.

Tonight I am reborn; tonight, she lifts the sorrow of this day so long ago and replaces it with joy, celebration, and happiness.

Thank you, my love. Thank you, my wife. Thank you, my universe.

# Love and Death

I sit in silence as I am being driven home. I look out the window. I can sense her thoughts and her presence. Shortly after, I receive a text from her, 'Our friends eagerly wait for you. But I eagerly wait to hold my husband. Hurry home to me, my love.'

I respond, 'I am almost home, and I eagerly wait to hold my wife.'

All I can do is smile. My universe wants me home, and all I want is to be home with her. To see her smile, smell her hair, and feel her lips against mine. I can hear her heartbeat as it grows louder as I get closer to her.

Gesture announces that an accident has occurred two miles ahead of us. I tell her to proceed with caution. As we get closer, I can see an image on the LED display that a lone vehicle is overturned and badly damaged.

I ask Gesture to stop the car. I get out, and silence is all I hear. Smoke billows out from the car. I walk around the car and see nobody inside. The frame of the car is collapsed from all sides. There are no skid marks and no indication of another vehicle being here.

I keep looking to see if brush anybody is still possibly in there. I begin to look in the dry think, patchy of the hill country to see if I find something, anything. Still, I can find nothing. I cross the road to continue my search, and it is the same result.

I am about to go back when I hear a moan, slight movement within the brush. I make my way to where I hear it. When I see it, I see that she is badly injured. Her face is cut up, her arms are ravaged with cuts and bruises, and she is bleeding profusely.

I immediately take off my coat and place it under her head. Using my watch, I ask Gesture to launch the drone and call 911 with video and the location of the accident. She is slowly waking up. She opens her eyes.

"Who are you? What happen?"

"Ma'am, my name is Ian. You were in a very bad accident. Is it just you that was in the car?"

"Yes."

As she tries to remember what happened, her body is no longer in a state of shock, and the pain is soon felt all over. She anguishes in pain; the tears begin to roll down her face. Her breathing becomes more rapid.

"I have some water in my car. Let me go get it."

"NO, NO, please don't leave me! Please!"

"Okay, okay."

She is beyond scared. I reach for her bloodied hand. I gently caress it. "What is your name?"

"Dawn." She says as she fights back the tears.

"Dawn, help is on its way. You're going to be okay."

She begins to cry more. I wipe away her tears. I brush her hair back from her face. All I can do is comfort her until help arrives. I do this for several minutes, trying to soothe her. I tell her not to talk but to save her energy.

I ask Gesture for the ETA. Gesture responds within thirty-three minutes. I continue to calm her the best that I can. Her breathing is slowing, and her tears begin to dry. She turns and looks at me, "Thank you."

"For what?"

"For not leaving me."

She looks straight toward the sky, and her last breath leaves her.

I have never seen anyone die. I call her name, I shake her several times, but she lay lifeless.

"NO!" I shouted.

I begin to give CPR. I pumped her chest, breathed for her, and repeated. I called her name for her to come back. For fifteen minutes, I did this, and then another fifteen minutes more. She was gone.

I looked at her. I looked at her hand and saw her wedding ring. I grabbed her hand, "I'm sorry, Dawn."

I closed her eyes.

I could hear the Air Life above me.

As they loaded her into the helicopter, I was given towels to clean the blood from my hands and face. I gave my statement, and then I was released.

I got into the car. I sat there in silence.

"Gesture, are there any vehicles on the road in route to the residence?"

"GPS and satellite images show nothing at this time."

"Take me home. Reach top speed."

"Top speed of 183MPH, is this correct?"

Calmly I responded, "Yes."

The car began to drive, and I could feel the car glide smoothly as Gesture counted nearing the top speed of 183 MPH.

I arrive home. My shirt has her blood on it. My hands have her blood on them, and my face had remnants of her blood, even after I wiped it away. I walk in into my house.

All I want is to see her. All I want is to hold her. All I want is to kiss her. I say nothing to our friends. I ignore them completely. I search for my universe, and I see her. She is outside, smiling and laughing.

I cannot get to her fast enough. I go to her, I go to my universe. When I get to her, I pull her in so tightly without her even knowing. I begin to cry as I hold her against me. I begin to cry as I breathe her in. I begin to cry as I can hear her heartbeat.

I begin to cry because she is all I have.

# On the Seventh Day

I open my eyes, and she is there, wide awake, just looking at me. She smiles and touches the side of my face, "Good morning." She whispers.

"Good morning. How long have you been awake?"

"A few seconds before you."

"How I love waking up to you."

"And I with you."

We both get out of bed and walk into the enclosed shower. We wash each other, hold each other, and laugh together. But we always have that one moment in which we look at each other and have that one kiss where I caress her gently and kiss her lovingly.

I begin to put on my white t-shirt, but she takes it from me and puts it on instead. She laughs as it hangs a little off her shoulder and past her voluptuous thighs. I put on my boxers and remain shirtless. She smacks my ass, "I want bacon with fresh-cut fruit."

I chuckle, "Anything else, my love?"

She looks down at my boxers and licks her lips, "Maybe later."

She is like a kid in the kitchen. She tickles me as I fry her bacon. She steals a piece, takes a bite, and then teases Mena with it. My universe begins to run around the kitchen with Mena right behind her. She screams and laughs as Mena is jumping all over her.

After cutting her fruit, I pour us a mimosa and grab her cream from the fridge. She runs and sits on the counter. She is winded. I grab a piece of bacon and give it to Mena. My universe grabs her mimosa and drinks it in one gulp to satisfy her thirst.

She grabs her fruit and eats a piece of strawberry. She looks at me as she chews her fruit. She dips her finger in the cream and pretends that she is going to lick it, only to look at me and then smudge it across her cheek.

I laugh, "What are you doing?"

I grab a napkin and walk over to her. I stand in front of her. She slowly opens her legs. I step in closer. When I do, she wraps her legs around me. She looks up at me.

"Close your eyes." She says.

I can feel her touch run across my bare chest. She is gentle and soft as she runs her fingers from one side to the other. She grabs the waistband of my boxers. She draws me in closer. I can hear her breathing faster. I then feel the cold cream rubbed all over my face.

She laughs and pushes me away. I use the napkin in my hand to wipe away some of the cold cream. She continues to stand there laughing. Even Mena looks at me differently. I begin to laugh, "If I were you, I would start running."

"Old man, you can never catch me." She said with confidence and a smirk.

I put the napkin down, and I can see that she is ready. I immediately bolt towards her. She runs around the island. She laughs, "Come on, daddy, you should know better than to surprise me like that."

"That is not a surprise. This is." I jump over the island in a single bound. She screams with pure laughter. She runs hastily, and I give chase with Mena in tow. She runs upstairs and back into the bedroom. She jumps onto the bed.

She is again winded. She pretends that she is going to run, but my reach is too much, and I could easily grab her. I walk onto the bed. She sways back and forth.

"What did you say about this old man?"

Her shoulders drop, she is admitting defeat. She walks over to me, looks up at me, "Kiss me."

The cream still on my face and that of hers, I smile and kiss my beloved universe. She kisses me, and with my guard down, she throws her body on top of mine, and I am lying flat on the bed with her on top.

"As I was saying, you could never catch me, old man, unless I allowed it," She leans over, licks the cream from my face, and then kisses me, "Victory tastes so sweet."

All I can do is laugh and admire my universe.

For the rest of that Sunday, we never left the bed. We watched movies, ordered pizza, played checkers, listened to music, wrestled in bed countless times, and she even reenacted parts of movies based on my books.

From sun up to sundown, we never left the bed. We were two kids again, two kids that are madly in love with each other. She lays on my chest as I touch her hair softly. She strokes my chest softly. We say nothing as we watch the moon in the late night hour.

We fall asleep, but I can't wait to have another Sunday like this.

# Four

It is -5° C inside the hotel at all times. My universe and I walk around a section of the Ice Hotel in Sweden. The room is big with high ceilings. Ice trees are sculpted with branches that reach the top of the ceilings.

She walks around in pure amazement; I walk around in pure amazement of her. She touches the trunks of the ice trees. She is in another time, another planet, another universe. I walk parallel to her. I see her breath come and go as she walks the halls of the Ice Hotel.

She turns to me. She leans up against the wall. She is serious. "Talk to me." She says.

I look at this woman who is the most simple of a person but yet she exudes the most profound treasures that any man could hope to discover. I will speak to her. I will speak to her heart. I will speak to her mind. I will speak to her body. I will speak to her soul.

"Did you know that it has been proven that you can fall in love in a matter of four minutes?"

She turns her head slightly, "Really?"

"Yes. It's based on attention and attraction. Once you attract the person, you have four minutes to keep their attention."

She begins to walk away slowly, contemplating what I have just said.

"Body language and the tone of the voice is what you will notice."

She begins to pull her hair to one side.

"The eyes for one another are what comes next. If the attraction is so great, it is proven that each other's heart rate will beat in synch."

She begins to think about what I am saying as she bites down on her lip.

"The act of falling in love has begun. Science says that it is the equivalent of taking a dose of cocaine. The brain begins to produce a euphoria throughout your entire body."

She runs her hand across the ice.

"Hence, happiness is felt throughout, along with the familiar butterflies in the stomach."

Her breathing increases as I can see her breath in the air.

"Phenylethylamine is produced by the body. It's this chemical that produces our flight-or-fight response."

She stops.

"It's in this moment the heart will decide what it wants. It's in this moment that you will give in and strip yourself of everything to reveal your true love for this person."

She turns and looks at me.

"As the clock ticks down to four minutes, a touch from either person will release a chemical known as oxytocin. This is what completes the bonding process.

"All this in a matter of four minutes?"

"Science has proven it."

"So science has just explained why we fell in love?"

"No, because the four-minute theory is false when it comes to us."

She is confused.

"Could you not fall in love with me in four minutes?"

I walk over to my universe.

"No."

She is still confused.

"Ian?" She whispers

I touch the side of her face.

"I could not fall in love with you in four minutes. Four minutes is a measure of time that is too long to fall in love. When I first saw you, you did not see me, we did not see into each other's eyes, and we did not touch."

I begin to get lost in her blue world.

"My love, when I first saw you, I knew immediately that I wanted and needed you in my life. The very second your heart began to beat, it was only meant to beat for me. The very second you breathed life, you were only meant for me. The very second you opened your eyes, your eyes were only meant for me, and the very second you craved contact, it was only for me."

She begins to tear up.

"That's four seconds."

"Exactly. Not four minutes, but four seconds, and right now, even those four seconds are too long to keep me away from you."

I step forward, take my universe into my arms, and kiss her with such intensity that the ice begins to melt. I can feel her heartbeat, I can feel her soul, and I can feel her love. Four seconds is all I needed.

Four seconds…

# Meant

I see her as she sleeps silently this night. While I am at complete ease, I cannot sleep. The night is cool in our tent. The windows of the tent are screened to protect us from the elements of the African desert. The floor is laid with the finest of fabric, a writing desk, and a bathroom of bronze and black.

I am not thirsty, and yet I walk over to the desk and pour the blue bottle of Tynant water into a glass. I place the glass of water next to her. The condensation from the glass drips down. Two drops race against each other to the base. The drop on the right wins. I leave her in her slumber and gently open the silent sliding doors of the tent and step outside.

The night is unlike any other that I have ever seen before. I look up and the magnificence of the Milky Way galaxy as it is exposed before me. It is beautiful to see billions of stars in such order. As I look out at this more than 13 billion-year-old galaxy, I realize how small we are and how time is so precious for the ones we love.

Of all the planets in the universe, I ended up on the one planet that contained a woman that is my entire world, my entire universe, and the sole reason for my heart to beat. I continue to look to the heavens, and as I do, I see a shooting star. Three seconds later, a loud thunderous roar from the sky erupts as lightning shots across the skies. I close my eyes and wish up my shooting star.

I hear my name being called.

I open my eyes, and I am in bed. I look over at her, and she is in the same position as when I left her sleeping. I arise from the bed. Was I dreaming? Was I sleepwalking? I walk over and pour the Tynant water into a glass and set it next to her. I see two beads of water racing to the base. Before they finish, I know the one on the right wins. But I wait for the inevitable outcome anyways.

I step outside. I gaze upon the countless stars the Milky Way galaxy exposes on this wonderful and clear night. I begin to wonder how is it that I came to be on this planet with a woman that was only meant for me.

As I look up, I wait and wonder if it will happen. A shooting star is seen racing past the skies. I am frozen, for I have seen this before. I count down, 3, 2, 1, and the roar of the thunder is heard. I look to the skies once again for the lightning to stretch across the night skies.

Like a light switch, I see the brilliance of lightning above me. I step forward, I close my eyes, and wish upon my shooting star once again. I wish for the only thing I could wish for…

"Ian."

I hear the whisper of my name. I have yet to open my eyes in this darkness. Let me open my eyes and wish for what I have always wanted and for it to never end. I open my eyes, and I am still outside. I turn around, and I see her standing outside with a blanket wrapped around her.

I am without words. I look at her. I have seen but a few seconds of the future, but it's still a future that is with her, a future that was meant for only us. I walk over to my universe. She opens her blanket to me. I embrace my universe, and she wraps the both of us in her blanket of love.

I look down at her. I run my fingers across her lips and to the side of her face. I stare deep into her eyes. In her reflection, I see myself. I see what was always meant, a world in which it is only I that exists, a world in which she is my home.

I kiss my universe; I kiss her adoringly and embrace her devotedly. That is our future, this is what is written in stone and meant to be.

# November

I have donated billions of dollars to a number of charities and families. It was always so simple to just write a check, but writing a check was no longer an option in her eyes. We are downtown at the convention center a little past 2:30 A.M

I am wearing a blue apron with a white cap cutting celery, my first workstation for this early Thanksgiving morning. I look down from me, and I see her as she is basting and stuffing the turkeys.

Her group is smiling and laughing as they work on this day of giving. My group, not so much, but who could blame them? We were focused on cutting celery with a sharp instrument.

As more volunteers arrive, I am pulled from my first workstation and taken to where the bags of bread rolls need to be separated. I do as I am told; my group is much livelier this time. Greetings and Happy Thanksgiving is said to one another.

I look for her, but this time she is at another workstation where they are separating portions of the turkey meat and placing them in an aluminum tray. I focus on my task, but my eyes seem to always find themselves looking out for her.

I love this woman so much. I look at her with such admiration. I love how she communicates her kind passion with a smile, a laugh, or that look of intent when hearing a story. Her simplicity is what makes her completely amazing.

At last, many of us are on the floor serving plates to the many men, women, and children who are not as fortunate as many of us. I go around carrying a tray of food to each and every person that I see. I am greeted with such kindness that my emotions are overwhelmed.

I am hugged, kissed, and taken pictures with. I sit down with these wonderful people who are so hopeful about life no matter what life has thrown at them. For many, a good meal and a warm place to eat in peace is all they seek.

This is what writing a check does not see, this is what a check does not experience. She has blessed me with this opportunity to open my heart more so than my wallet, and it's something I wish I could have learned early on in my life.

I am in the back washing dishes, something I have not done in some time. Yet, I find myself smiling and my heart full of love. I feel a tap on my shoulder. I turn, and she is there with two plates of food. I dry my hands and walk with her.

There is nowhere left to sit in the kitchen. Many more volunteers began to arrive. We find a corner, flip over two buckets and use them as chairs. She places the food on my lap. She begins to unfold my napkin and place it on my lap as well.

She reaches over and picks up two cups filled with tea from the floor. She has served hundreds of people today, and yet she still continues to serve me before herself. I look at this woman who opened my heart in more ways than just one.

I lean over and kiss this life that I call home. I adorn her with so much emotion that, once again, time stands still. I can feel the blood rushing to her lips to garnish my love with hers. With the cups still in her hands, she wraps her arms around me and encompasses me with her love.

On this day, I give thanks. I give thanks for my one true love that continues to instill in me what it is to give and receive. On this day, I share my universe in a time of giving.

# A Mothers Loss

We float on a body of icy water in the middle of the Northern Hemisphere. The sun is beginning to set, and almost instantly, the temperature begins to drop to -10°F. The drop in temperature is immediately felt. It was a clear sign that Mother Earth is not welcoming us this night.

She has every right to give us the cold shoulder. She is old and battered, and yet she continues to provide. She begins to howl loudly. Winds begin to scream through the caverns of the glaciers. She speaks of anger; she speaks of sadness and the heartache she has had to endure.

As Mother Earth ravages the north with her threats, I see Sky walk to the front of our boat. She stands there in silence. She closes her eyes. She is a statue of pure beauty and enlightenment.

The winds quickly surrounded her. Blowing her hair from side to side. I see her brace herself against the onslaught of these powerful winds. While she is doing fine by herself, I can no longer watch this attack. I come from behind and shield her with my body.

She continues to stand there in silence. She is the definition of focus and determination. As she begins to open her eyes, the once-angry mother is no more. She looks at the pure beauty of the icy blue glaciers.

Till now, nothing could ever rival the deep blue of my universe. The glaciers are enormous and deadly. They sit behind one another, ready for the next attack brought on by us. But this time, it is us who would like to stand on her side and help defend them and protect them.

More boats arrive, boats that carry scientists, engineers, doctors, teachers, and even musicians. My universe pleads for us to help her. Mother Earth is tired, she lets her guard down, and when she does, an ear-cracking sound begins to come from her. There is silence when suddenly another ear-piercing crack is loud and thunderous. This was not a sign of violence, but a cry for help, a cry for help that may be too late. We watch the massive side of the glacier begin to fall into the sea.

She had been holding on to that for millions of years, and in seconds, it was lost forever. We are but one mile away from her face. Water and ice hit the side of the boat, swaying us from side to side. The event is not violent but sad as we watch her slowly disappear from existence.

We are lowered into a smaller boat and begin our journey to her. We come to a glacier that is easily two hundred feet tall. She comes to the side of the behemoth. She reaches over and touches the gentle giant with her gloved hand. She pulls back, takes off her glove, and again places her hand on the glacier.

She sheds a tear for her. She closes her eyes and bows her head in silence. She is paying respect for her loss. She looks to the top of the glacier. She nods her head.

We are returning back to the boat. She comes over to me, and I engulf her with my body. She looks up at me, "Tell me you will help save her."

I look into the deep blue of her soul. I kiss her on the forehead, "With all that I have."

I have all the resources in the world at my disposal, but the one resource I do not have is time. It is the bidding of my love and the bidding of our love for the planet that we must succeed or perish trying.

So it begins…

# Christmas Lights

After dinner downtown, we walk the Riverwalk. It's the last night in November, and It's a cool 33°F outside. I let her grab the back of my arm as I walk on the side of the river to protect her from falling in. I guide her. She is all smiles tonight. Her beautiful glow is ever so powerful.

We say very little to one another, but on the inside, we are professing our love to each other as loud as we can. As I walk, she rests her head on my arm. I look down at her and kiss the top of her head. With a touch ever so soft, she squeezes the back of my arm.

We walk slowly on this beautiful clear night. The world around us is passing us up as if we were standing still. Everyone around us was in a rush, including that of the water. Why rush this moment between two people that are truly and madly deeply in love with one another?

Sometimes when love is so powerful, it will cause the universe to pause and reflect on this wonderful union between two loved ones. It's rare, but it does exist, as we are living proof of that love. Although we walk among many, we are in great company as he watches from above.

I take her underneath a tree on the river. I turn to her. I look at her. I let her look deep inside my soul. I am inviting her to penetrate me with all the love she has for me.

She does so with immense power, and when she does, the people around us began to disappear, and the ticking of the clock begins its countdown to the stoppage of the universe.

I take in a deep breath, and I feel her love radiate throughout my body. It is powerful, maybe even a little too powerful for me at times. But I will not falter, her love is all that I want and accept.

She has done it.

She steps out of my soul and back into hers. She looks around. We are alone. She looks at me in pure amazement.

"Is this real?" She asks.

"Come here."

She comes into my world. I touch the side of her face, she closes her eyes. I lean in and give her a kiss. A kiss so powerful it shoots across ancient galaxies of the cosmos.

When we pull our lips from each other, she opens her eyes. All around us, Christmas lights are wrapped from tree to tree, from branch to branch, and from bridge to bridge.

She was in awe of the beautifully strung-up lights that surrounded us this night. She walks and spins around, enjoying the beauty of the lights.

While our surroundings are beautiful, I could not stop looking at her and her happiness. I can see her heart and soul with such joy and love.

Her happiness is my happiness, her love is my love, and her soul is my soul.

Merry Christmas, my love. Merry Christmas.

# Out of this World

The morning is calm, and the cool wind is felt across the Montana skies. I stand on a little over 300,000 acres of which I own, and bought for one sole purpose. In front of me is a massive building that spans twelve miles long.

I stare at the heavens and admire this beautiful day. Nia comes alongside me, "Isn't it the most magnificent thing you have ever seen?"

I turn to her, "Not quite. How is she?"

"Gesture shows that she is fine." She hands me a tablet, "Would you like to see her?"

I grab the tablet and watch as Mena is searching her new surroundings. "Has the outside been exposed to her yet?"

"No. I'm sure you want to be with her when we do."

I smile, "Thank you." I give her back the tablet.

"What about Sky? Do you know if she took the sedative?"

"I left her instructions to take it thirty minutes prior to arriving here. I was told by one of the pilots that she had taken it, but it took some convincing."

"I'm sure it did, but it's better that she is at ease when we commence our journey."

"I agree."

I see the helicopter approaching in the distance. I look at my watch, she is right on time. The helicopter lands on the helipad. The rotors firmly blast my clothes against me. I open the door, and she is blindfolded, as I had requested. I carefully help her down.

"Good morning, my love," I lean in and give her a kiss.

She is all smiles and giggles. "Can I take the blindfold off yet?"

As much as I want to see her beautiful face, I tell her that it is not time. I take her hand and place it behind my arm. I begin to escort her into the building, a building that is truly one of a kind in the entire world.

We walk into the building. It is cold, and the echoes can be heard as I continue to guide her further into the building. A door slides open, and within is a subway train that travels throughout the complex. "Almost, my love, almost." I sit next to her, and Nia takes her place behind us.

The subway glides at an incredible speed, but it is barely felt from the inside of the cabin. For three minutes, we sit in silence. I touch and caress her hand with mine. I have dreamt of this moment for so long. Now my dream is a reality.

We arrive. I again place her hand behind my arm. We step off the subway, and greetings from my BlackStone family could be heard from all over. She is all smiles as she tightens her grip.

My dream is but a few feet away. I can feel my heart double its beats. I take off the blindfold. She smiles at everyone there. My family of BlackStone surrounds us, and with love and kindheartedness, even Nia walks over and hugs my queen.

"Where are we?"

"Soon, my love, soon."

Nia walks over to me, "Are you ready?"

"Lead the way."

We walk behind her, and our families continue to clap and holler. Today is a defining moment for the company, but my defining moment is the love I show her every day. We walk into a large oval capsule. Inside the capsule is a spacious seating area that can accommodate thirty-three individuals. But today, it will just accommodate my universe and I.

"Do you trust me?"

"Always."

"Nia, please commence the countdown."

"Of course, Ian. You two have a safe trip."

"Trip? Ian, where are we going?"

"In time, my love. I promise to show you."

Nia walks out, and the black doors close behind her. The locking mechanism is loud as it is in place and sealed. I walk over to her, "We should probably sit down."

She walks over to me and sits next to me. Once she does, a slight jolt is felt. She grabs onto me. I ease her fears and hold her against me. "It's okay, I would never allow anything to happen to you."

She looks deep into my soul. She finds comfort from within me. There is no safer place in this world than with me. I touch her hair softly. Again, she finds comfort in my touch. She closes her eyes and enjoys each stroke.

We are in synch once again. I can feel her body go limp as she puts all of her weight on me. She is asleep, and maybe for the better. I continue to touch her. As I do, I begin to relive the memories that we have shared together.

I smile at every memory that I think of. I smile and begin to wonder how is it that I am so lucky to have been blessed with a woman like her. I had never known what love is or what it felt like until I met her. She breathed life into me.

She brought me from out of the darkness and into her light. With no fear, she plunged into the depths to show me that we are meant to be. She would fight till her last breath in order to be with me, and I, too, would fight to be only with her.

I kiss the top of her head and continue to touch her hair. I love this woman so much, so much that I want to give her the world, and even then, that's just the beginning. I place her hand inside of mine. I can feel the warmth of her hand.

I close my eyes and listen to the most majestic sound, that of her heart. I can feel it pulse within her and through me. The beating of her heart comforts me as I close my eyes, and I, too, fall asleep holding on to her.

We have arrived as I hear the locking mechanism disengage, and the doors begin to open. I gently wake her up. "We are here, my love."

She slowly gets up, "Where is here?"

I grab her hand, "Let me show you."

We exit the capsule and onto a multi-tiered complex. She lets go of my hand and walks around the massive complex.

"Where are we?"

We are greeted by Gesture. A video screen is pulled up. Nia comes on. She smiles, "Hello, guys. How was your trip?"

"It was fine. No issues at all."

"Good. Gesture is monitoring your vitals, and they are all normal."

"Good, that's good to hear."

"If you should need anything, just give us a holler."

"Thank you, Nia, and thank everyone for Sky and me."

"Of course. Sky?"

"Yes, Nia?"

"Take care of him."

"Always."

Nia smiles, and the video screen disappears.

"Ian, where are we?"

She walks around the multi-tiered complex. The layout is all black with silver and dark bronze accents. She walks over to the elevator.

"How many floors is this place?"

"17."

"What is this place? Where are we exactly? Are we still inside the building?"

"Technically, we still are."

"Ian, I really am confused."

"I know. Gesture, locate Mena."

"She is en route to you. Would you like a video of her?"

"No."

"Mena is here too?"

"Yes. Actually, she has been here for a few hours. I thought you would want her with us."

She smiles, "Ian, I am so confused right now."

"All will be unveiled shortly."

I can hear her dog tags chiming as she makes her way down the stairs. She immediately runs over to her mother and I.

She stoops down to pet Mena. She is so happy now that her mother is here with her. I watch as she strokes Mena softly, lovingly, and adoringly. There is only good in her, and because of this, I want to give her everything that I can.

She stands up and continues to stare at her surroundings. Even though this is my first time here, I cannot help but keep my eyes on her. My eyes follow her around the huge complex. The black marble is so clean and transparent that I see two of her. One in the present and the other in another time and dimension.

I take my spot in the middle of the vastly huge complex. I call her. She turns and looks at me. She begins her journey to what will be the most historic time in human history. Mena follows her and sits right next to her.

I look down at my dog, my beloved daughter, and my best friend. She, too, will go down in human history. She was once a stray, a runaway, but now she has a family, a family that completely adores and loves her.

I turn my attention to her arctic blue eyes. Oceans from across the universe could never be so pure and clear like her eyes. I dive into her world of blue. I find comfort and solace as she allows me to enter her soul.

I look at every inch of this glorious universe. Everywhere I look, I am breathless, and yet it is not air that I am starving for, for I am absolutely calm. I starve for something else. I starve for her touch, her words of passion, and her never-ending love.

I could only have dreamed of such a place or written books about it, but now, at this very moment in time, I am staring at more than a dream come true. I am staring at a destined bond between a man and a woman who hold the keys to each other's true love.

It is time to end this chapter, the first chapter in our lives. It's time to turn the page and begin our next chapter.

I step forward, and I place my hands on her face. Her skin is so soft, and her beauty is unmatched. From within, I tell her it is time. I tell her that I love her more than anything humanly possible.

I ask her to close her eyes. I ask her to stop time once more, for this time will be our forever moment.

The ticks of time are slower and farther apart. I feel both of our hearts begin to slow.

I kiss her soul, I kiss her heart, I kiss everything, as I could do this for an eternity.

I whisper to her soul, "Open your eyes."

She slowly opens her eyes. She immediately puts her hands over her mouth. She looks all around, and her reaction is the same… speechless. Even Mena is sitting in stunned amazement. And again, while this is the most stunning thing that could happen to a man, woman, child, or animal, I still give my eyes to her.

She turns to me, she is crying tears of joy, tears of happiness, and tears of rejoice, for I have brought her home.

The black darkness from the windows are now peeled back for her to stare out of. She turns around and stares in the vast openness of space, for we are 60,000 miles above the earth in what is called a 'Space Elevator.' I come from behind her; I place my hands across her waist and hold her next to me. Mena sits in front of us.

We stand together in the test of time. We stand together as we are each other's strength. We stand together so that the universe can finally get a closer look at the ones who define true love and family.

It has been a long journey for the three of us to cross paths. Each one of us was broken along the way, but we finally found each other. When the story of us is told, it will have been the greatest love story in human history.

It will be seen, it will be heard, and it will echo for an eternity throughout our universe.

We finally made it.

We are finally home among the moon… and the stars.